Writing is one of those remarkable passions where an author is privileged to enter emotional experiences that enable personal discovery. I have written since I was a little girl, exploring the relationships of family life, the complexities of growing up in a post-war Hungarian refugee family, the dramas of the wider world.

I often write about the people I love, the events that have touched me, my past and my present. My children and my nieces and nephews have always been and continue to be an important reason for my writing. I so greatly want them to make sense of the world, which at times is difficult and confusing. I want them to find inspiration and fulfilment and discover that the world is wonderful.

*Butterflies* has been a personal journey of discovery where I entered into the lives of burn survivors and found humour, courage and hope. That is what I want those who read my books to discover themselves. That is why I write.

SUSANNE GERVAY

Other books by Susanne Gervay

*Next Stop, the Moon*
*Jamie's a Hero*
*Shadows of Olive Trees*
*I Am Jack*

# SUSANNE GERVAY

# Butterflies

Angus&Robertson
An imprint of HarperCollins*Publishers*

Special thanks is given to Dr Hugh Martin for the time he generously donated in assisting with the medical advice in the writing of *Butterflies*. Special thanks is also given to the remarkable doctors and staff of The Burn Unit, The Children's Hospital, Westmead, NSW.

While all characters who inhabit *Butterflies* are fictional, the inspiration for *Butterflies* is the courage of all those who have passed 'through the fire'.

A percentage of all sales of *Butterflies* is donated to The Burn Unit Trust Fund at the The Burn Unit, The Children's Hospital, Westmead, NSW.

### Angus&Robertson

An imprint of HarperCollins*Publishers,* Australia

First published in Australia in 2001
Reprinted in 2001
by HarperCollins*Publishers* Pty Limited
ABN 36 009 913 517
A member of the HarperCollins*Publishers* (Australia) Pty Limited Group
http://www.harpercollins.com.au

**HarperCollins*Publishers***
25 Ryde Road, Pymble, Sydney, NSW 2073, Australia
31 View Road, Glenfield, Auckland 10, New Zealand
77–85 Fulham Palace Road, London W6 8JB, United Kingdom
Hazelton Lanes, 55 Avenue Road, Suite 2900, Toronto, Ontario M5R 3L2
*and* 1995 Markham Road, Scarborough, Ontario M1B 5M8, Canada
10 East 53rd Street, New York NY 10022, USA

National Library of Australia Cataloguing-in-Publication data:

Gervay, Susanne.
Butterflies.
ISBN 0 207 19850 0.
I. Title.
A823.3

Cover photograph: International Photographic Library
Cover design by Lore Foye, HarperCollins Design Studio
Printed and bound in Australia by Griffin Press on 80 gsm Econoprint

7 6 5 4 3 2    01 02 03 04

*Like butterflies, those who survive burns*
*defy their fragility to migrate large distances*
*and find warm climates.* Butterflies *was written*
*for all those heroes who survive burns and for all those*
*special people who help them on their great journey.*

# CHAPTER ONE

Jessie, don't you just think Mr Roberts is the best English teacher?'

'If you say so, Katherine. It's so hot I really don't care.' She slings her schoolbag over her shoulder. 'This bag is heavy. I've got that much homework to do tonight.'

'We all have. Can you stop complaining?'

'I'm not, but it's stinking weather and I do have a lot of homework.'

'Are you going to the Horror Festival, Jessie? The original *Dracula* is showing this Saturday.'

'I saw *Frankenstein* last week. Pretty good for an old movie. Yes, I'll go and see it, if I finish my *Romeo and Juliet* homework. I hate Mr Roberts. He sets that much work.'

'I like the way he reads *Romeo and Juliet*. "But soft! What light through yonder window breaks? It is the East, and Juliet is the sun."'

'Well I don't.' Jessie smiles suspiciously at Katherine. 'Is it Mr Roberts or *Romeo and Juliet* you're so interested in?'

'That's not worth an answer, Jessie.'

The usual group of senior boys waits at the bus stop. They've got their shirts half unbuttoned and their ties undone. It's been a hot February in Sydney. Two weeks of heatwave conditions and the temperature is still 40 degrees. Sweat drips off Marc's forehead as he clowns around, pulling out William's shirt, kicking a few bags, telling disgusting jokes.

Jessie likes Greg, the tall, skinny, red-haired one standing next to Marc. Katherine elbows her. 'It's him.'

'Shush.' Jessie gives her that 'don't you dare say anything' stare.

'Girls … girls coming,' Marc calls out. 'What do you call ten girls standing ear to ear?' There are snickers. 'A wind tunnel.'

'You're the wind tunnel, if you ask me,' someone calls out, but it doesn't stop Marc. The heat, the end of the school day, his mates laughing, egg Marc on.

Katherine trips over Jessie's bag as she drops it. 'Sorry.'

Marc mocks her. 'Can't keep on your feet.' He stares at her. 'God, it's Dracula,' he laughs. 'You'll have to hide yourself in a paper bag if you want to get love at first bite.' Marc smiles at his cleverness. Some of his mates laugh.

Katherine looks up at him, her face flushed. Jessie grabs her arm. 'Why don't you shut up, you idiot,' Jessie yells at Marc. 'Who'd even bite you? Not Dracula, that's for sure. He wouldn't want blood poisoning.' There is sniggering.

Jessie whispers, 'Don't worry about him, Katherine.' As the bus pulls in, she says aloud, 'Marc's a pain in the neck.'

Everyone laughs.

Contemptuously, Jessie taunts him. 'Why don't you get a life, Marc?'

'Sure thing, as if you'd know what a life is.' Marc reddens as he runs his hand through his hair.

'It's all right,' Katherine lies. 'I don't care.' The hot air makes the eucalypts crinkle and crack in the summer heat. She glances at the trees through the bus windows. *I've got to pretend, pretend, pretend.* Suddenly, she looks away from the cracking leaves with their broken skin. *Why did he say that? Think that? What have I done to you, Marc? I was happy today.* She watches him slouch into a sticky bus seat, sweating humidity and male scent. *I'm not going to cry. I won't give you the satisfaction.* 'Yeah, why don't you get a life.'

Marc looks at Katherine quickly, pulls off his tie, then turns to discuss rugby results with his mates.

Jessie sits next to Katherine in a back seat. 'Don't worry about him, Katherine.' Jessie points to her neck. 'Anyway, look.' She touches a small scar just above her collar bone. 'I've got this.'

Katherine stares at the small scar with its fine line. She rubs sweat from her eyes and turns away. 'It's so humid, Jessie. They say there'll be storms tonight. Can you study in this heat?'

'I've got to study.' Jessie reverts to complaining about school subjects, teachers and examinations. Katherine half listens as she watches the boys occasionally punch each other, occasionally look around at the girls, leering and joking. She stares at their thick black shoes scuffed with kicking and tripping each other, then she kicks the seat in front of her.

The bus stops. Katherine steps out onto the sizzling bitumen footpath, deformed into potholes and striations. She waves to her friends then runs from the bus towards home, sweat dripping down her shirt into the small of her back.

She unlocks the front door. On the kitchen bench are the breakfast plates with the remains of toast and jam. Black ants are crawling between the strawberry jam and melted butter. *Suppose I'd better clean it up before Mum gets back.* She throws her bag into her room, hitting piles of books and CDs she's left scattered on the floor. Then she goes back to the kitchen.

The sink. *Cold water first. Cold, then hot.* The words are habitual, repetitive, persistent. The cold is a relief. Slowly, carefully, she turns on the hot water, letting it flow gradually into the cold until the sink is full. Suds slosh as she rubs and swishes plates and knives and spoons into a bubble bath of reflections. *Hide in a paper bag. Hide. Hide.* She stops, rubbing her sudsy hand along the right side of her face, down her neck, her arms, feeling the ripples of taut skin. She has heard the story so many times that she isn't sure if it is her memory or theirs.

*Katherine is nearly three. Chubby and brown eyed. There are photographs of her then. She's pretty. Mum is so young. Katherine's playing with her big sister Rachel on the front lawn outside the units. The oleander trees are pink. She loves the pink flowers but they're dangerous. People get allergies from those trees, blow up with rashes and welts.*

*Right next to the oleanders, there is a red-brick pit.*

Shuddering, Katherine shakes her head. She dries the plates and stacks them inside the cupboard. She goes to her bedroom, shoves clothes and mess to one side, then puts on her CD. Hard rock blasts through her room and between her books. Hard rock blasts into the house, blasting so that no one can hear her crying, softly at first, then louder. Louder.

'Turn down that noise,' Mum shouts as she drops shopping onto the table. 'Katherine, it is too noisy. Put the music lower.'

Her sister, Rachel, carrying more bags, follows their mother into the house. 'That's a horrible sound.'

Turning down the volume Katherine calls out: 'It isn't horrible. You're so boring, Rachel.'

'Boring! What's wrong with you, Katherine? You're in a rotten mood.'

Katherine's long hair hangs over her face so they can't see she's been crying. 'Nothing's wrong, except you. You live in the Stone Age. Haven't you heard of good music?'

Rachel rolls her eyes. 'Yeah ... right. Whatever I listen to, at least it isn't hard rock. That's really the end.'

'End? As if you'd know.'

'Will you two stop fighting and help me get the dinner ready?' They don't stop and they don't help. 'That is it. These marshmallows are going to hit you girls in a minute.' They ignore her until ... plop. Marshmallows soar into the air. One just misses Katherine. Two hit Rachel on her head. They stop fighting. Their mother is laughing. '*Bene, bene.* You look like fish with their mouths open.' Her slight Italian accent makes the words sound like laughter. 'Do not worry, you can still eat the marshmallows. They are not damaged. Now, come and help or no food. Look what I bought for you two. Your favourite — mangoes, very sweet.'

Katherine is quiet as she unpacks the groceries while her mother and Rachel gossip and prepare dinner.

'I'm starving,' Rachel announces as she brings the pasta to the table. 'Come on everyone. Dinner's ready.'

'Yes.' Their mother smiles as she digs the serving spoons into the salad. 'Old Mr Jones does love his salad, especially with the baby tomatoes. You know he has a very strong grip. At his lunch, he held onto his fork while stabbing the tomatoes. One landed on his cushion, and when he lay back — squash.' She's laughing now. 'Tomato sauce.'

'Mum, you're mad.' Rachel bites into a tomato.

'That is what they say at work too.' She stops laughing. 'I like looking after the people in that community house. I wish for a permanent job there.' She fiddles with her coffee cup.

'Who else would do that job? Who'd want to work in that crazy place?'

'It is not crazy, Katherine. I do not like you saying that. The people there need help and I need the work.'

'Those people want to be there, want to be helpless and sick.' Katherine pushes away her dinner. 'Not like me.'

'They are not sick. You know that. They need a little help for a while.' Her mother puts down her coffee cup. 'Are you all right?'

'Mum, she's just having one of her scenes. Why don't you grow up, Katherine. You're ruining dinner.'

'Well, I'm so sorry.'

'Stop it, Katherine.' Her mother looks at her daughter. 'Is everything all right? Was it school? Did something happen?'

'No.'

Her mother waits. Stares at her. Puts her hand on Katherine's arm.

*Don't touch me. I don't want to be touched.* But she doesn't pull her arm away.

Rachel stops eating and stares too. Katherine looks away from them, confronting the kangaroo paw with its furry pods. *What are you pointing at, you stupid plant? There's nothing to point at. Can't I be in a bad mood if I feel like it? Stop staring, Mum. Stop it, Rachel. You're staring a hole into me. Are you all going to just watch me? Are you afraid that if you stop looking at me, someone'll take me? You're wrong. Wrong. No one wants me. No one will ever want me. That's what he said. In front of everyone. I've got to hide. Do you want to hear that?* She stares back at them. *All right then, I'll tell you. A plain, brown paper bag that people stuff their leftovers into then put in a garbage bin. That's what I am.* She holds her stomach as if she's going to be sick. Then shakes her head. *No. No, I can't tell.* 'There's a fair bit of pressure from school work. It's getting to me, that's all.'

'You are better off than the people in the community house.'

*I don't need a lecture, Mum. I can't make it, if you lecture me. Not today. Please, Mum.* Katherine gets up.

'Katherine. You do know you are lucky?'

*Lucky, lucky me.* Katherine shrugs. 'Yes.' *I want to go now. Let me go.* Katherine stands looking down at her mother.

'Katherine, you have choices. Many of the people in the community house have not such choices yet.'

*You try, don't you Mum?* 'You're right. Mum.' *I don't want to argue today. It's hot and it's too hard. I hear what you're saying, but I just want to look normal, like everyone else, that's all.* 'I've got to study.'

'You've always got an excuse for not washing up,' Rachel complains.

'Your sister has to study if she wants to make the university.'

Rachel rolls her eyes.

'It is only until the end of next year.' Their mother wipes down the table.

Katherine disappears into her room. *Studying. I hate it. What's the point of reading and re-reading the same notes. Memorising things I already know. There are so many other things to learn in this world. I don't understand why ...* Scribbling on a notepad, she gets her pen to work. She flips open her maths textbook. *Why? Scribbly little numbers. I want to scratch you out.* Dark blue lines cross and re-cross the notepad until Katherine's fingers hurt and the paper is torn with holes and pen marks. *Okay, okay. Calm down. Katherine, think. Think. I'm going to be a doctor. Focus. A doctor. That's the reason. Then all this'll make sense. I just need to breathe deeply, control myself. I know, I'll put on some music.* She sifts through her CDs, leaving the hard rock aside. She finds the shiny silver disc.

Carefully she blows fine dust from the disc, then inserts it into the CD player. The deliberateness of her movements, the concentration on the physical act is calming. Waiting for the music, she crouches on the floor next to the player with her head bent over her knees. The melody wafts through the room as she slowly traces the lines of her body with the palms of her hands.

Last month, just before school started, Katherine went with her sister to see the red-brick pit. They had been there twice before. Once with their mother a long time ago and once on Rachel's sixteenth birthday. It was hard. They cried standing over the red bricks, grieving as if the pit had been a grave.

Katherine and Rachel talked many times about going back to see the pit, but there were always excuses. Study, friends, the hospital. This time it was different. No excuses. Katherine was starting senior school, Rachel was starting work as a dental nurse and their mother was employed in the community house. Their lives were beginning to make sense.

'We have to go and see it now, don't we? Just you and I?' Katherine asked.

'Yes.'

Katherine stood in her black, laced shoes on the brick edge of the pit. A rusty metal grate was welded onto the top now, but they could still peer down through the bars. Leaning over the pit together, they saw sunlight disappearing into a black hole.

Katherine shuddered, then defiantly shook her head. 'You're not so important are you, pit?' She kicked the edges of the bricks, scratching marks into them.

'No, not important,' Rachel repeated.

They both knew it was a lie.

Tears shimmered in Rachel's eyes. 'Mum never blamed me, but Dad did.' She wiped her face. Touching Katherine's arm softly, she took a breath. 'I need to tell you here, right in front of the pit. It ... it's so hard to say, but you have to believe me. You're my sister and I love you. I would have saved you if I could. I wanted to save you.'

'I know.' Katherine awkwardly put her arm around Rachel. 'You're my sister and I love you too.'

*'You did it, didn't you? You pushed Katherine.'*

*'I didn't, Daddy. I didn't, Daddy.' Rachel's pale cheeks go red and tears wet her seven-year-old face.*

*Rachel doesn't like her Daddy's loud voice.*

*He grabs Rachel's head, forcing her to look past the oleanders at the red bricks. Just a square in the ground. Charoal wood and burnt firelighters lie in disjointed piles inside it. The pit isn't beautiful now, with its bright lights and dancing flames. There's an aluminium lamp attached to a wall near the pit. Rachel turns her head towards the lamp. The tall, reddish-haired man doesn't let her look at the shiny aluminium with its silver reflections. His heavy hand pushes her head close to the pit, past the red bricks.*

*She can just make out bits of the the earthen floor lying deep under the soot and ashes.*

*Deep inside the pit. Deep.*

*Katherine had been playing, grasping for the dancing flames, when she tripped. They engulfed her small arms and she fell into the pyre of garden refuse and chemical fumes. She screamed for Rachel and Mama. The gardener ran to her. They all ran to her. But the petrol burnt fiercely. Acid flames covered Katherine's brown hair and her head, burning her hair, her face, her body. Acid flames covered her arms and her little body's chubby folds and soft baby skin.*

Katherine turns the page of her maths text, relieved to leave the algebraic equations. Geometry. She likes working out the problems, making the circles complete and the geometrical lines cross and join into perfect prisms and pyramids. There are answers, solutions. *There has to be a point for the pain. The awful pain. There's got to be an answer.* She presses her fingers against her lips. *I know there are miracles. The Professor said there are miracles. I'll have soft skin and pretty hair one day. One day, I'll wear my hair up. I'll be like everyone else. One day.*

She looks out of her window into the backyard where her mother's parsley and the orange marigolds grow. *The lawn needs mowing.* Katherine focuses on two kookaburras perched on the washing line. *Laugh kookaburras, laugh. Please laugh.* It's as if the plain brown and white birds hear her. They suddenly start laughing and playing on the washing line pegged with sheets and Rachel's white shorts. The birds laugh and laugh until their long triangular beaks look like smiles and their ordinary feathers sparkle with streaks of blue hidden beneath their wings. *You're beautiful. Beautiful.* Katherine touches her hair, which is long and straight now. *Thirty-seven operations. Will I ever be beautiful? Will anyone ever want me?* She forces herself to turn away from the kookaburras and focus again on her maths.

Next morning, Jessie waves at Katherine as she enters the schoolyard. '"She speaks, O speak again, bright angel, for thou art, As glorious to this night..." Well, it's day, so I won't go on with that quote. I'm exhausted. I studied *Romeo and Juliet* all night. I might even get as good at it as you are.' She smiles. 'But I'm still not in love with Mr Roberts.'

'Very funny.' Katherine walks with Jessie towards their lockers. They talk about last night's homework and study and the heat, until Katherine says, 'You know yesterday, on the bus with Marc and his mates?'

'Don't bother about them. They're stupid, that's all.'

'Jessie, listen. I have to bother about them ... and about other things.' Jessie looks at Katherine. 'We've been friends for a long time.' Katherine waits for a moment. 'Are we good friends?'

'Of course we are.'

Katherine lifts her hair exposing the scars, exposing her neck and her shoulder. 'Can you see that?'

'Yes.' Jessie shifts uncomfortably.

'Is it the same as the scar above your collar bone?' Katherine touches Jessie's small scar, making her jump backwards. 'Is it thick and rough and hard in places, and grafted with new skin again and again?' Katherine's brown eyes are dark, challenging Jessie. 'Did you get third degree burns on fifty percent of your body?' Shivering, she speaks deliberately, slowly. 'And the surgery and vomiting afterwards and the pain and no father and your mother crying with you?'

'No,' Jessie whispers.

'Girl who has to hide. Girl who no one will love. That hurt. A lot. But it was terrible when you compared what I've been through with your tiny scar.'

'I didn't mean it. I just wanted to make you feel better.'

'It made me feel like nothing. I may be ugly, but at least I don't want what I've been through trivialised. Then I'm really nothing.'

'It's not trivial. I admire you. You're smart and you *are* pretty, Katherine.'

'Sure I am. Pretty as a princess.' Katherine rubs her hands. 'Marc and his friends laughed at me.' Tears edge into the corners of her eyes. 'I want to look like you. I want your little scar to be mine. I want a father to take care of us and my mother not to work so hard and the scars to disappear so I'm like you.'

'Don't be like me, Katherine.' Jessie bites her lip. 'I didn't think. I don't know anything. I'm sorry.'

'I want to be a kookaburra.'

'What?'

'A kookaburra.' Katherine wipes the palms of her hands. 'It doesn't matter.'

'I'm really sorry. You're my friend. I never want to hurt you.'

Katherine nods.

# CHAPTER TWO

Rachel fiddles with her sister's long hair. 'You've got split ends. Have to cut them off.'

'Hey, not too short. Watch those scissors. Are you cutting too much?'

'I'm not. Stop moving around.' Rachel pulls at a few strands. 'It'll look great for the dance.'

'I don't know if I'll go.'

'Don't be stupid. You've been talking about it all month. And why did I make the silk braid to thread into your hair? It took me ages to make.'

'You know you like doing crafts, so it wasn't such a big thing.'

'That's gratitude for you. I could have made something for myself you know?' Rachel shakes her head. She's very particular as she cuts each strand carefully, trimming, fiddling, styling before she threads the braid into the long plait that hangs over the side of Katherine's face. Rachel glances at the photograph that's been on the mantelpiece for as long as she can remember.

*Katherine is sitting on Santa's lap holding Small Pup, her fluffy, toy sheepdog. She's wearing a white cotton dress with chocolate dots that match the colour of her eyes. There's a cream satin bow in her hair. It hangs over her left ear. On the right side and along the back of her head, there is no hair.*

*In the hospital, her mother had been furious at those other mothers who concealed their children's scars under hot jumpers or huge hats, making the children sticky and afraid. She attacked them. 'Those burns are part of your babies. You have to accept the burns if you accept your babies.'*

*As if in defiance of those mothers and the people who wanted their children to hide, she insists that Katherine wears a bow in her hair for the Santa photograph. Rachel is wearing a bow too. It's yellow.*

*'But Mama, I've got no hair. Everyone can see, Mama.'*

*'Katherine, you cannot hide your scars or you will be hiding forever.' Mum pulls her cream jacket around her, then bends to kiss her little girl's scarred head and the side of her face without hair. Her voice quivers just a little bit. 'I love every part of you. You are beautiful, Katherine. Make sure you smile for the photographer.'*

*'I don't want to smile, Mama.' Her face scrunches into a frown and the satin bow wobbles. A big boy stares at her half bald head and Katherine dives at him, giving him a huge bite on his arm.*

*'My sister is strong.' Rachel giggles as the boy runs off to tell his mother. The boy's mother looks up to see their mother standing with her arms crossed and Katherine with no hair. She doesn't say anything and Katherine is smiling when she goes up to Santa.*

Rachel shakes her head, remembering Katherine taking a chomp out of the boy or anyone else who stared at her.

'What's so funny? Have you wrecked my hair?'

'Right, as if I would.' She points to the photo. 'Katherine, do you remember when that picture was taken?'

'Sure.'

'You were really cute. Santa nearly had a heart attack when you asked him for some hair for Christmas.' They both laugh. 'Santa looked really stupid not knowing what to say. Mum whispered something in his ear and then he told you that you'd have long hair one day, but not this year.' Rachel plays with the braid. 'You got so angry, you know.'

'But I have hair now.'

*Fluid pumps under Katherine's scalp, making her head wobble like a freakish growth. And then there's the cutting, the dragging of the stretched skin*

*across her head, the draining of the fluid and pulling
of her growing hair over her baldness. The pain is
terrible. Four years of operations. In hospital,
Katherine holds tightly onto the small, stuffed
sheepdog that's been with her ever since the
accident; been with her into every operating theatre,
and lies with her at night in bed. Small Pup has bald
spots too.*

*As the trolley moves towards the operating theatre,
she screams, 'I'm scared. Scared. Mama, help me. Why
are you letting them take me?' She calls out again and
again until the anaesthetic works and her mother cries
at the glass doors that separate them.*

'Okay. Have a look in the mirror, Katherine.' She
jumps up and runs to the bathroom.

Katherine screams out, 'This is great. Great. You're
definitely the best braid-maker. For a dental nurse.
Ha! Ha!'

'Very funny.' Rachel smiles at her sister. 'You
know, dental nurses can have other talents.'

At lunchtime, everyone is talking about the dance.
Jessie is excited. 'Katherine, remember, we've got to
make the guys go crazy when they see us. I've
bought this blue skin-tight satin top that'll look
fantastic.'

'It'll go with your blue eyes. You look great in
everything anyway.'

'I don't think so.'

They gossip about music and teachers and the dance until Katherine half stammers: 'Marc. Do you think he'll be there?'

'Who cares if he is or isn't? He's an idiot.'

'But what if he is?' She blushes. 'All his friends heard what he said, you know, on that day. Everyone thought it was funny.'

'Katherine, you can't let him or his friends stop you from doing what you want. I'll be there and you know I'll have a rotten time without you. So, you've just got to come. So, you're coming. Right?'

Katherine doesn't answer at first. Then she looks at her. 'I guess I will.'

The bell rings and they go to their Physics class. The summer sun beats through the open windows and it is hot and humid. Katherine feels the tightness of her skin under her right arm. *I need another graft.* She rubs her leg, unconsciously massaging the stinging out of her thoughts. *I hate grafts. But I want to be able to move. I'm supposed to be happy about that. Moving my arm. I guess I am. I still hate them.*

*Rachel is sitting on her sister's legs while their mother grabs the cream. 'You're not putting that on me, Mama.'*

*'I will smack you if you do not keep still.'*

*'The doctor said you can't smack me. It'll wreck the graft. So you can't, Mama.'*

*'You keep still, Katherine.'*

*'I don't have to. It hurts.' She pulls away from her mother's hands calling out. 'Hurts. Agonia, Mama.' Italian words slip between her English as Katherine fights against her. 'A lot. Molto, molto.'*

*'I know it hurts but ...'*

*Katherine gives Rachel a huge kick that knocks her onto the floor.*

*'Stop it, Katherine. Stop it, Katherine.' Her mother reaches for Katherine's good arm. 'There is no graft here.' She pulls her daughter too hard, digging her hands into Katherine's smooth skin, pressing too hard, holding, unable to let go. Katherine is sobbing but her mother cannot let go.*

*'Mama, Mama, you're hurting me.'*

*Suddenly she releases her hold. She stands for a moment confused. Then she puts her arms around her daughters and starts to cry softly. 'I am very tired, bambine. I am sorry. Sorry. Sorry.'*

Jessie nudges Katherine as she picks up a pen. The teacher is droning on about formulas and atomic structure. Jessie conscientiously takes notes. She wants to be a physicist. Katherine shifts uncomfortably. *My skin's so tight.* She traces the graffiti of initials carved roughly into the wooden desk. Shuddering at the roughness, she puts her writing pad over the graffiti. *What will I wear to the dance? I've got nothing to wear. I'll look ugly. I don't want to be ugly.*

Jessie's long, blonde hair is tied back into a ponytail that flicks over her shoulders as she writes.

*You're a good friend, but you'll never really understand.* To cool her neck, Jessie lifts her ponytail, letting the air seep between her soft skin and her hair. *That'll never be me, will it?* Katherine shakes her head and tries to listen to the teacher.

At last school ends for the day. The weather is still hot, sticky, and the doorknob feels wet as Katherine unlocks the front door. She looks in the kitchen and her mother's bedroom. *Mama, where are you? Mama, come on. I want to talk to you. Please, where are you?* She knows her mother is at work. She got the permanent job as an assistant. She'd been happy about it and Katherine had tried to smile. 'All the time I spend in the hospitals, in the rehabilitation and burn groups with you, Katherine. It is not going to be wasted.' Laughing, she'd added, 'I even will be allowed to arrange the flowers. I love to do that.'

Katherine bites her lip. *I wish you still pushed me in the stroller, delivering leaflets or doing odd jobs or cleaning. At least you were here for me.* Sometimes, when she was little, Katherine used to go with her mother to clean people's houses, scrubbing the bathtubs and stainless steel sinks of wealthy women and not so wealthy working mothers.

'*Come on, Katherine, be a good girl. Bring me the broom. We must hurry up. I do not like leaving Rachel at home by herself.*' Katherine carries the broom precariously, making her mother laugh.

'You are a good girl.' Her mother's black hair is swept back into a bun, the way she always wears it. Her clear olive skin, brown eyes and lilting accent mark her as Italian, but she's Australian now. Wisps of hair escape as she leans over the broom to sweep the kitchen floor before washing it. 'I like doing a good cleaning job for Louise. She is always kind to us.' Mum squeezes detergent into the bucket. 'She likes you, Katherine. It is nice, what she gave you.' Katherine admires the white socks with frilly lace at the top. 'I have told her many times not to buy you things.' Mum's sweating as she mops the tiles. Katherine watches her.

The kids at school have been teasing her about her mother. Katherine defended her, shouting at them that Mama isn't just a stupid cleaner. She had kicked a big girl, making her cry.

'Why do you clean Nina's house, Mama, and the houses of other people? I don't like it.' Her mother stops washing the floor and turns to look at her eight-year-old daughter. 'You can be a secretary in an office, Mama. You can wear nice clothes and drink cups of coffee and tea. You don't have to clean toilets. It's embarrassing.'

Her mother's dark eyes are ice, but what she says burns into Katherine's mind. 'Yes, I am a good secretary. I can write letters, answer phone calls, drink coffee, but that is not what I do. I am not embarrassed, ashamed. I will never be ashamed of cleaning toilets. Is that what you said?' Katherine stares at the floor. 'Cleaning toilets? I clean them and I scrub the garbage bins and I would clean the footpaths if I have to. Do you understand why? Look at me, Katherine.' Her mother waits until Katherine raises her head.

'I clean because we need the money and because I cannot work in an office, going in every morning and working all day. Cleaning fits in between those times you need me — when there are operations or when I have to spread cream over you all through the day or when the graft splits away or when the graft works. I am there for you, Katherine.'

She never asks her mother again about the cleaning, but afterwards, when her mother cleans, she takes a duster and dusts all the shelves.

Katherine looks for Rachel. 'Where are you?' Rachel's room is tidy, her nightie neatly folded on her quilt. Rachel's still at work. *I'm sick of it. Everyone's gone. Unfair. Unfair. Just leave me, that's right. No one's there any more to tell off those kids who call me ugly or Bald Eagle or Mashed Potato or some other rotten thing. You used to be there for me, Rachel. I don't want you to leave me alone at school or alone on the bus or alone at the dance. Everything's unfair.*

It is still hot and her school clothes stick to her back. Katherine throws her school shoes into the bedroom and strips off her uniform and tosses it into the room too. She catches her reflection in the bedroom mirror and stops to stare. Her skin is tight. The smoothness of her left side merges into skin which looks like the broken leaves of dry eucalyptus trees. She presses her hands against her breasts. She had cried when she got her periods and her breasts had tried to grow. Rubbing her hand over her left breast she rolls the nipple into hardness, kneading the soft tissue. Her right breast is different. She'd been fourteen when they'd transplanted tissue from her thigh to her breast, slotting it under her taut skin but there wasn't a nipple. Maybe she'll get a nipple one day. Slamming the bathroom door shut, she turns on the cold water.

'Hello, Katherine. We are home.' Her mother arrives with Chinese takeaway and Rachel's brought home three sets of false teeth to practise her dental work. She's studying part-time to be a dental technician.

Katherine is in her shorts and T-shirt. It's cooler now with the evening breeze. She stands, watching them from her bedroom doorway. 'You actually got the car started? That's good. Well, a miracle really.'

'Hey, are you criticising my car? It runs very well you know.' Rachel stands up straight, defending her first car. She's saved most of her pay for it. A twelve-year-old sedan. On Saturday afternoons she takes Katherine out, driving really fast over humps and potholes and they scream and laugh together on the back roads.

'No, no, great car.'

Their mother sets the table while Rachel fiddles with a pair of false teeth. 'Dinner is ready, Katherine.' Her mother looks up, then smiles. 'You must be hungry.'

Katherine walks to the table. 'Smells good, Mum.'

Rachel shows Katherine the teeth. 'What do you think? A full clean treatment or braces or a plate?' She smiles. 'What about pulling them all out? The teeth I mean. The gums can stay.'

Picking them up, Katherine shakes her head. 'I definitely like the gum look. Pull out all the teeth.'

Rachel laughs. 'Great idea, except no teeth means no work. Will you help me? I have to write a report on my proposed treatment and you're good at writing.'

'Compliments get you everywhere. All right.' Katherine runs her fingers over the teeth. The Chinese food smells delicious. Her mother chatters about work. Rachel puts the teeth on the bench.

*I'm happy. You're home now, you're home.*

CHAPTER THREE

*Hairy ripples cover her. Her bald head snarls with threatening teeth like a hyena. It's the Beast. Too terrible. The Beast.*

Katherine jerks open her eyes. Two-thirty in the morning. She rolls over onto her stomach, reaching for Small Pup. *I'm too old for you, Pup.* She feels his worn patches and presses him against her face. *I don't care.* Tucking Pup under her arm, she closes her eyes.

*The Beast can't talk, but shrieks at the shining Prince, who's dark and handsome. The Prince isn't afraid. He opens his arms and holds the Beast, caressing, soothing until the Beast no longer shrieks. 'Your fur is velvet,' he murmurs, putting his lips against her fur, whispering 'beauty' until the Beast purrs and her ripples begin to disappear. Soft, brown hair flows down the Beast's shoulders and her skin becomes pale and smooth. The Prince calls her Princess. He calls her beautiful. The Beast isn't a beast any more. It has a name. Katherine.*

Spoken words disturb Katherine's dreams like they've done for as long as she can remember. She calls out in her sleep.

*Katherine doesn't speak after the accident. She used to say, 'Mama. Rachey. Play with me. No. Brava. Chocolate.' She sees the speech therapist, who is kind and makes her form sounds, but there aren't any words. Katherine's mother practises words with her, but she still doesn't speak. Rachel plays dolls with Katherine and talks for her sister.*

*Once her mother shouted at Katherine, 'Speak! Speak! Say anything. You can. I know you can.' Katherine garbles sounds, grunting out noises, grunting until her mother shakes her, until she holds her tightly, until her mother is crying.*

*Katherine is five, playing with Rachel in the playground on the swings and seesaw and climbing bars. She's climbing the metal bars, right to the top, even though it's hard to stretch to the next bar. She pulls with her right arm and her chubby face strains with effort.*

*Her mother is talking to a friend on the park bench. She glances at the girls in between discussing recipes and ex-husbands. 'Katherine, you're too high,' she calls out.*

*Katherine looks down for a moment, then reaches higher. Her right hand tips the bar as she grasps for it, forcing scars to pull, scars to tear apart. Like a ball she crashes and rolls and bounces, calling out, screaming, 'Mama, Mama, Mama.'*

*Katherine's arm is broken but she speaks after that. The doctor says it's because of the shock. The speech therapist says she's just ready. The counsellor says she learnt that her mother and sister can't do everything for her. She has to talk herself.*

'Hurry up, Rachel. I need a shower now. I'll be late for school.'

A teasing laugh trickles out of the keyhole. 'You'll just have to wait. Ever heard of that?'

Katherine bangs on the bathroom door.

'Stop that noise.' Their mother shakes her head as she pours herself coffee.

'Oh, Mum, by the way, I'm going shopping with Jessie after school. She's got to get some shoes for the dance for next Saturday. I haven't anything to wear, but I saw something at The Fashion House. I'll use the birthday money Nonna and Grandpapa sent from Italy.'

'The shower's empty,' Rachel calls out.

'About time.' Katherine races into the bathroom, slamming the door. The sounds of gushing water and Katherine singing blare through the house.

'She never stops talking.' Her mother smiles.

\*　\*　\*

'I thought I wouldn't make it to lunchtime.' Katherine eats her salad sandwich and olives as she and Jessie wander up the hill to their group's regular lunch spot. 'I was starving in Biology. I was so desperate I was actually thinking that the dissected frog looked pretty delicious.'

'That's disgusting. You're obviously dieting *again*. Katherine, your ten-day diets, your grapefruit and egg diets, your ... what was that other diet? That's right, the Israeli Army diet. They're ridiculous. Bet you didn't have breakfast.'

'Maybe I did have breakfast, maybe I didn't.'

'You didn't and you always end up starving and scavenging for food.' Other girls says hello as Katherine and Jessie sit down between them.

'I don't scavenge.' Katherine looks into Jessie's lunch bag. 'Can I have some of your dried apricots?' Katherine chomps into an apricot. 'Scrumptious. Better than a green slimy frog.' She eats another one. 'I wish I was thin, like you.'

'Come on, you have a fantastic body. You're not going to look like those super-thin models, but you look great.' Jessie takes an apricot too. 'And the way you're stuffing yourself with my apricots, I don't think you really want to.'

'Can we NOT talk about dieting? Just become a vegetarian like me, and you'll be fine.' Liz doesn't wait for objections and starts talking about the Horror Film Festival. 'Did anyone see the last film of the Festival? *House of Wax*. Vincent Price was great as the burnt sculptor. He was demented, killing people so that he could make them into waxworks.'

'Definitely more interesting than diets.' Julia scrapes her fingernails across her pencil case, making them all scream, 'Stop. Stop.'

The diets are forgotten as they argue and giggle over haunted houses, werewolves, Dracula, corpses rising from the dead. Horror movies twist and turn, weaving between apricots and olives.

Katherine shudders, trying to stop thoughts of burnt hands and body snatchers. *I can't take this today. I just can't. Talk about something else.* Katherine interrupts determinedly. 'Hey, what's everyone think about the dance on a harbour ferry?'

Julia tries to finish her story about a vampire sucking blood, but can't compete against the dance.

'What'll I wear?' 'Who's going?' 'The harbour?'

'It'll be great. Sea breezes … it would be too hot to have a dance in the hall. We'd be disgusting and sweaty.' Liz finishes her apple and puts the core into her lunchbox.

'You know why it's on a ferry?' Julia smiles knowingly.

Lounging back on the grass, Jessie asks, 'Why?'

'It makes it a dry disco. No alcohol. I bet the teachers will frisk the guys getting on board.'

Jessie grins. 'I'd like that job.'

'Very funny. Some of those guys aren't going to like the alcohol ban.'

'So what? They'll have to live with it. We're worth it, aren't we? Anyway, I'm definitely not interested in alcohol and throwing up. That's what some of those losers did last time.' Jessie looks at her apricot. 'Just the thought of it turns me off my lunch.'

Katherine untucks her shirt. It's wet with perspiration.

'Anyway, the guys will be trapped on the boat,' Liz adds.

There's a malicious laugh from Jessie. 'With *us*.' They giggle about the boys and which ones they like and what's funny about them until the bell goes.

Mr Roberts returns the class essays on *Romeo and Juliet*. 'That was excellent, Katherine,' he says as he hands hers back.

Hiding a smile, Jessie nudges her. '"Parting is such sweet sorrow, That I shall NOT say goodnight till it be morrow."'

Katherine kicks Jessie under the desk.

The bell goes and there's the scraping and pushing of chairs under desks and the sound of books slamming shut. 'Last class today, Katherine, thank god. It's so hot.'

'I've got swimming training tomorrow morning. Wish I was swimming tonight.'

'And why did you kick me in English class? It hurt.'

'As if you don't know why.'

'All I was doing was admiring the secret but, of course, great romance of Katherine and Mr Roberts.

Mr Roberts, Mr Roberts, where art thou, Mr Roberts?'

'Very funny.' Katherine tugs Jessie's ponytail. 'You're pushing it. Can we forget Mr Roberts for a while? Are we going shopping?'

Jessie packs her bag. 'Yes, of course. Shopping. Shopping. We've got to sacrifice ourselves, trudging tirelessly, heroically through shops. We have to look gorgeous, hot or not.'

Katherine's laughing. 'You'll have to be an actor. Forget Physics.'

'Sure.' Jessie taps her watch. 'We've got serious shopping to do and we really haven't got much time. Let's go. My dad gets really angry if I'm home late. I can't stand him sometimes.'

'Come on, your dad's all right.'

'He's not. You should hear him shout at Mum and my brother and me, especially after he's been working all day in that great and wonderful law firm. You'd think it was a prison camp, the way he goes on.'

'At least you've got a dad.' Katherine swings her bag over her right shoulder.

'Sure.' Jessie shakes her head. 'Everything has to be exactly how he likes it. One day ...' Jessie shrugs. 'You want to go to The Fashion House don't you? They have some great clothes.'

'One day what?'

'I don't want to talk about it. Let's have some fun. Look, the bus.' They race to the bus stop just in time to scramble up the steps of the bus. Marc's at the rear with his mates. He looks up at Katherine. She quickly sits down, turning her back on him.

'This is the tenth shoe shop we've been into, Jessie. I don't think there are any more shoes to try on.'

'You're a bit dramatic. Who's the actor now?' Jessie slips on a pair of black shoes.

'They look great. Buy them.'

'Are you just saying that to get out of here?' Jessie flicks her ponytail.

'No. Well, yes, but they do look fabulous.'

'Are you sure?'

Katherine nods.

'Very sure?'

'Yes. Yes. Yes.'

'Okay. I'll buy them.' As she pays for her shoes, she looks at her watch. 'There isn't much time and we've got to get your dress.' She bites her lip. 'I've been a bit selfish, I think.'

Katherine looks at her seriously. 'You're right.' Then she laughs. 'Come on then, Jessie. We've got to move. Let's get to The Fashion House before it closes. Lucky for you that I know what I want.'

They run all the way, panting as they fall through the door of the boutique. 'Air-conditioned, thank god.' Katherine goes straight to one of the racks. She pulls out a strapless black velvet dress. 'It's beautiful, isn't it?' Stroking the fabric, she shivers with anticipation. 'I love velvet.' She heads for the change room. 'I hope I fit into this.'

'Of course you will, even though you ate nearly all my apricots.'

'As if I did,' Katherine laughs.

The shop assistant asks Jessie how everything is going. 'I'm waiting for my friend. She's looking for a dress for our dance.' They wait for Katherine to emerge.

'I'm here.' She swirls around so that her long, brown hair spreads out in a whirlwind.

Jessie laughs.

The shop assistant watches uncomfortably and plays with her grey leather watchband. Katherine swirls around again. The shop assistant murmurs, 'There's a wide selection of dresses to choose from.' She moves towards to the clothes racks and carefully selects a dress. 'What about this one?' she stammers. 'That dress you're wearing doesn't look quite right, don't you think?' She holds out a plain, black cotton frock with long, dark sleeves and white buttons right up to the neck.

Katherine reddens. Instinctively she rubs her hands along her scarred arms and up her neck, then stares defiantly at the shop assistant. 'No. I'll take this strapless dress, thank you.'

# CHAPTER FOUR

'Come on, Katherine. Come on.' Her mother's and sister's voices tunnel through the water, urging Katherine to swim faster, faster. *Come on. I can do it. Just push yourself, Katherine. Push. Strong strokes. Fast strokes.* She's tailing the swimmer on the right. *I only need an extra second.* There is screaming as Katherine edges towards the other club's swimmer. *I can see you.* Closer ... *push, Katherine, push ...* Equal ... *I can do it. I can. Can.* Equal ... *keep going, touch the wall, stretch, faster, stretch, stretch* ... The wall. There's cheering. Second place.

Katherine punches the air with her left arm, rips off her goggles, then takes a dive. The salt water stings her eyes. *Second place. Smile, Katherine.* She smiles, waves to her club's supporters. 'That was wonderful,' her mother calls out from the edge of the sea pool. Katherine looks past her mother to the surf crashing against the rocks. Her mother's voice is insistent, forcing Katherine to turn away from the sea. 'You were wonderful.' *Wonderful? Am I, Mum? Second place. That's not wonderful. I don't want to be second. I can't be second if I'm going to make it.*

'It was a pretty good time,' Katherine lies. She wraps a towel quickly around herself as always, avoiding the stares of strangers before she joins her team-mates. The coach is preparing everyone for the relay, talking about last-minute strategy and teamwork. Katherine will be the second swimmer. While she listens she rubs the towel against her back, then under her arm. Staring at the towel, she suddenly shoves part of it behind her. When everyone's attention is on the coach, she feels under her right arm. It's sticky. The skin is broken. A tear. Her stomach knots. *I don't want this. Please. Please.* The ocean breeze is warm and the evening air hot and steamy, but her teeth chatter. *Why do I keep trying? Why do I pretend that I can do it? Me, a winner? I'm* ... She presses her hand against her lips, forcing the trembling to stop. *I'm not like everyone else.*

The water is rough blue, smelling of salt and sea, so different to pale blue surgical walls smelling of antiseptic and gauze. *A graft. That'll mean two months out of swimming.*

The coach interrupts her thoughts. 'Katherine, did you hear what I said? You've got to go out fast.'

'Yes.' *A graft. The hospital.* She rubs the back of her leg. *A graft will mean I'll miss the season. The practice sessions. All those mornings Rachel's driven me to the pool. She'll kill me.* But Katherine knows her sister won't kill her, and she knows something else. The scars under her arm won't stretch. Katherine looks at the coach. *I'm slower. The race.* Her right arm had pulled against the burns as she pounded the water in unbalanced strokes. *It was so hard. Freestyle. Except nothing's free for me.* She grits her teeth. *Everything costs for me. Mum says I'm lucky. I hate her saying that. I don't feel lucky.* Katherine starts breathing deeply, trying to stop the growing panic. *Calm down, calm down. I swam tonight, didn't I? I just have to swim faster next time, train harder.*

The coach walks with them to the starting blocks. 'To win this race you have to focus. Focus on your stroke, turns, kicking, pacing. There shouldn't be anything else in your mind. The mind is as important as the body.'

Carefully padding towards her block, Katherine stares at the grey concrete. *Focus ... turn quickly, push.* Her feet drag against the gravelly bits. Ripples tingle down her back and she shudders. She looks up. The last reds of the day stretch over the evening ocean. White manes crash onto darkening sand. *I can't focus on kicking and pushing water and gravelly concrete, Coach. But you're right. The mind is important, but it's not like you say, Coach. I don't want to focus on the way my feet drag along concrete, the way my arms splash through water. There's got to be more. When I swim, there are no concrete walls. I swim right through them, out into the ocean, like the dolphins. They're so beautiful and fast. Champions. No. I won't have a graft. Not here, not now, because I am a dolphin tonight.*

Rachel, Katherine and their mother walk towards the car. Kids wave, parents carry towels and goggles, the sound of water drifts between onlookers and participants.

'I am very proud of you, Katherine,' their mother says. 'First for the relay. Second for your own race. We will ring up your nonna and grandfather. They will be so proud of you too.'

Katherine nods.

There's a jerk forward as Rachel clutch-starts the car. 'A bit of a problem with the starter, that's all.' Concentrating on the gearstick, she methodically manoeuvres the car through the traffic.

Katherine watches the gearstick jerk left, right, vaguely hears her sister's foot move between accelerator and brake, listens to her mother mumble about service stations and swimming. Hot air blasts through the car window, cutting the stifling heat. Katherine's long hair flickers in the wind like strands of sticky honey.

Rachel stops in the driveway with a satisfied grin. 'Made it.'

They enter the lounge room, which always smells of flowers and kitchen herbs, like their Nonna's stone house clinging to the cliffs above the Ligurian Sea. Hand-blown Venetian glass and a white marble figurine sit beside red kangaroo paw in an Australian earthenware pot.

Katherine slouches on an old stuffed armchair as she reaches for the phone. 'Nonna, I can't hear you. Yes ... the line is clearer now. Yes, I'm happy that I came second. My time is fast ... Yes, I'll swim for my team ...'

Then her mother takes the phone. Her soft Italian relates the events of her life in Australia as she reconnects herself with her parents and that other life that is still part of her.

Katherine listens for a while, catching gossip about the Napolis who moved to Rome, the good weather and the huge crop of olives this season in the groves among the hills.

Three Christmases ago, when most of Katherine's hair transplants had been completed, when her hair camouflaged scars and striations, they went to Italy. Grandfather had sent the tickets and they'd flown for twenty-three hours right across the world. Rome for a day. Their mother had taken them to St Peter's Basilica. Katherine remembers wandering with her sister and mother through the baroque colonnades that led to an expansive piazza. She'd caught her breath when she saw the magnificent Basilica, but it was Michelangelo's *Pietà* that made her cry. Michelangelo's statue of a mother who seemed like a girl, cradling her dying child, who was a man. *Is life like that? Does it hurt so much?* Katherine put her arm through her mother's then. Afterwards they bought one of the many copies of the *Pietà* from the souvenir stalls that surround the square. Their *pietà* had been more expensive that the cheap imitations in plastic and bronze. Katherine had selected a small white marble figurine.

They stayed a month in their grandparents' village on the northern coast, looking out towards the island of Corsica. Katherine felt she'd always known the village. When she was a little girl, before she would fall asleep, her mother would gently speak Italian and tell stories. Stories about growing up among medieval walls and castles, and pine forests and olive groves that descended into fishing villages of blue harbours and netted sands. Somehow those stories were part of their mother and Katherine.

'Papa, my home is Australia,' their mother said to her father, blushing with confusion.

That Christmas, donkeys climbing windy, narrow streets, old widows in black, beautifully dressed girls coming home from Milan, and markets filled with food and flowers, pushed Australian beaches and hot sun into another time. On Christmas day, scents of holly and mistletoe mingled with warm cooking as doughy *cappelletti*, hot chestnuts and lentils wafted throughout the house.

They had been part of a family with aunts and uncles, first and second and third cousins and stepcousins and grandparents. Grandpapa had sat at the head of the table.

*I miss ... I want ... need ... I don't know. Something that was there in Grandpapa's house.* Suddenly she thinks of her own father. Katherine's mother said that he left them after one of their terrible arguments over money and children. 'I'm never bloody coming back,' he'd shouted.

Her father visited Katherine once in the hospital.

*Katherine looks like a mummy with white bandages wrapped around her head and chest and leg. Rachel is sitting on the hospital bed with colouring-in pencils and a large drawing book. Katherine grabs a blue pencil and draws a wobbly bow on Rachel's carefully coloured-in yellow horse. 'Don't,' Rachel shouts, grabbing for the blue pencil. 'I'm telling Mama when she comes back.'*

*'What's going on here?' a deep voice asks.*

*They stop and look up at a man with reddish hair and checked shirt, black trousers and big boots. He's carrying a box of chocolates.*

*Katherine's eyes light up. 'I like chocolates.'*

*Rachel's blue eyes are dark and scowling.*

*'How are you, Rachel and Katherine?' he asks awkwardly.*

*Rachel nudges her, whispering: 'Don't speak to him.'*

*'You can't tell me what to do, Rachel.' Katherine smiles and her chubby cheeks glow. 'I'm good. Do you know my mama?'*

'Yes.' He pauses. 'I've brought you chocolates.' He moves closer to the bed to give her the box. 'I am ...' he hesitates, then looks at his shoes. The sharp scent of male aftershave clashes with the lingering fragrance of their mother's talc and perfume.

Rachel stares determinedly at the linoleum floor. Katherine takes a caramel chocolate. The man watches them for a while, then leaves before their mother returns.

'I hate him.' Rachel snatches her picture of the yellow horse from the bed and sits in the corner of the room.

Katherine looks at her sister curiously, then chooses another chocolate, a hazelnut whirl. 'Yummy. Do you want one Rachel?'

'No.'

*Hazelnut whirls. I don't like them much.* Bed is cool with newly-washed white sheets that smell of clean soap. Rachel calls out 'goodnight', as she turns off her light. Their mother tinkers in the kitchen, clattering dishes. She calls out, 'Sleep well, bambine.' Katherine turns her bed lamp off and puts Small Pup beside her. ''Night.' The house is quiet, Katherine's bedroom door shut, the room closed to intruders. She closes her eyes cautiously. *I don't want to dream. I don't want to dream,* but water splashes through her thoughts until she's swimming, endlessly trying to catch the swimmer in front.

\*   \*   \*

The next morning Katherine is tired as she walks through the school gates. Jessie's standing there waiting for her. 'How was the swimming meet?'

'All right. First in the relay.'

'That's great.' Jessie isn't really listening. 'Guess what? Guess! You can't guess.'

'Probably not. You're going to tell me though, aren't you?' Katherine drops her bag down onto the black bitumen. 'This is heavy.'

'My bag is too.' Jessie's nearly breathless. 'It's Greg. He asked me to the dance. He's just the cutest, most sensitive guy. Everyone knows that. Should I go with him? Should I?'

*What? The dance?* 'Greg? What do you mean?'

'Aren't you listening? He's asked me, can you believe it? Me, to the dance.'

*Listening? You're going with me, aren't you? I can't go without you. Greg? Aren't you my best friend?*

'Katherine.' Jessie tugs Katherine's sleeve. 'Are you all right?'

'Yes. Yes. Greg. That sounds like great news. You've liked him for ages.' *Like him? What about me? Do you like me?*

'Well, I haven't said yes to him yet, because I had to ask you if you minded. There'll be all the other girls there at the dance. You'll know everyone. Will it be all right?'

*No ... No, it's not all right. It's wrong. Didn't we buy your shoes together? What about my black dress? I'm scared of going without you. You know that. You said you wouldn't go without me ... and Marc will be there.*

'It'll be fine. I'm glad for you.' *I want to go home.* 'Look, I've got to get some books from the library before class this morning, so I'll see you at lunch, if that's okay?'

'Sure. You promise you don't mind about me going with Greg? It's just that if I don't go with him, he'll ask someone else. Then he'll probably never ask me out again.'

'I said it's fine. I've really got to get to the library.' Katherine walks quickly to the library, then past the library, up the stairs, up more stairs, up to the out-of-bounds roof area. There's only Justine there, smoking against the railing. Katherine ignores her and slumps against a wall. Sliding down the rough brick face, she sits with her head bent over her lap. Rubbing her hands up her thighs, up her sides, along her arms, her neck, her head; she explores the ripples that are part of her. *You'll never leave me, will you? You come with me everywhere. Everywhere. Jessie. Jessie, I trusted you, like I trust my sister and my mother.* The bell rings.

At lunchtime, Jessie talks about Greg until everyone groans. 'All right, all right. He's fantastic.'

'I know you love apricots. Do you want some?' Jessie flourishes dried apricots in front of Katherine, making some of the girls laugh.

'No thanks. I don't feel like any today.' Katherine bites into her salad sandwich.

'Since I'm going with Greg, Katherine can go with one of you.' The girls chatter, talking about where to meet Katherine before they get on the cruise boat.

*This is so humiliating. What are you doing, Jessie? Why do you think you can organise my life? Just so you don't feel any guilt about letting me down? Well, feel the guilt.* 'Honestly everyone, I'll be right. I'll get there if I want to. What's everyone wearing anyway?' That's all they need for conversations to change, crisscrossing between clothes and make-up and guys.

Rachel is making dinner tonight. She's good at cooking because she's been doing it since she was a little girl. Her mother had to be with Katherine in the hospital. That's when Rachel got used to unlocking the back door with the key, taking off her school uniform, doing her homework, putting on her dinner, then watching television until her mother came home and she felt safe to go to bed. Her mother would leave dinner packets that Rachel could just heat in the microwave oven, but later she learnt to cook ravioli, lasagna, scrambled eggs, even pesto tortellini. Tonight she's making spaghetti with homemade bolognaise sauce.

'Needs a bit more basil.' Rachel stirs the potful of bubbling pasta sauce.

Katherine stands over her sister. 'I've come to inspect. Looks good.'

'Of course.' Even though Rachel is twenty-two, her freckles and bobbed reddish hair make her look younger. She taps the pot with her big ladle. 'Ready or not.' They sit around the table, passing parmesan cheese, pasta and sauce, pouring lemonade into glasses, sharing the serving, complimenting Rachel as they twirl spaghetti onto their forks.

Their mother puts down her fork. 'I feel so sorry for Jack in the community house. He is only eighteen and no one will visit him.'

'What's he there for, Mum?'

'Rehabilitation from the drugs. I hate to see young people ruin their lives, and that Jack is a good boy.'

'You're a really kind person, Mum. I'm lucky to have you as my mother.' Katherine looks at Rachel, adding: 'And you as my sister.'

Rachel laughs. 'You didn't say that yesterday when I told you off about leaving a mess in the bathroom.'

'It wasn't that messy.'

'It was. You left your wet towel on the floor and the toothpaste lid off. I just hate that. Anyway, forget about the bathroom. Something's happened because you're being too ... what's the word? Sentimental. That's it, too sentimental.'

'Nothing's happened. Can't a person appreciate her family?'

Her mother hides a smile. 'Yes, that is very nice. We like being appreciated. Katherine, is there something else?'

A waft of garden scent trickles through the back door, mingling with the cooked pasta. Katherine breathes in the smells of her home. 'How come friends just let you down?'

'Friends?'

Katherine fiddles with the spaghetti.

'Leave the spaghetti alone, will you?' Rachel sprinkles parmesan cheese onto her meal. 'So are you going to tell us?'

'Maybe I will or maybe I won't.'

'Well, get on with it.'

'Rachel, it'd be great if you listened for a change.' Katherine hesitates. 'Nothing's happened. It's just that I've got so much studying and training to do, I haven't got time for the dance. I didn't want to go anyway. It was Jessie's idea.'

'But you've bought a dress for it,' Rachel interrupts. 'And what about the terrific braid I made for your hair?'

'I love the braid. I'll wear it some other time. It doesn't mean I have to go to the dance just because of it. That's ridiculous. I needed a dress anyway, so that's not the point.' *I can't go. I can't. Who would want to dance with me? No one. Jessie'll be with Greg. I'll stand alone in a corner and everyone will dance or talk, except me. What can I talk about anyway? Grafts? Operations? My scars? My hair? I want to wear my hair up. Why can't I even do that? I'm not going to the dance. Marc'll be there for sure. What if he calls me something awful? What if he says I should hide in a paper bag again, in front of everyone? That's me, girl who has to hide. I want to go to my bedroom.* 'Jessie's found someone else she wants to be with at the dance. Greg.'

Her mother pushes aside her bowl, then looks up at her daughter. 'Katherine, I want you go to the dance.'

*I'm scared. Really scared. Please, Mum. You don't understand. You can't even see what I really look like.* 'Mum. No.'

'Is it because Jessie is with this Greg?'

'No,' Katherine lies, 'but she isn't much of a friend, is she?'

'I do not know that.'

Katherine shrugs.

'I think you should be there with your school.' Her mother speaks softly. 'Do you want to run away? If you do, then you will always have to run. I do not want that for you.'

*I don't either, Mum. But I can't go.* 'I'm not running away, Mum.'

'Please Katherine, promise to think about it. I would like you to go.'

Katherine motions that she'll think about it, then gets up from the table and takes her plates to the sink.

# CHAPTER FIVE

*The Beast is swimming in the blue sea, pushing, struggling against whirlpools of water sucking her downwards. Rachel is driving her beaten-up car along the sand, calling out, 'Where are you? Where?'*

*Flicking her ponytail in the air, Jessie's dancing in her new shoes, heels so high she looks five metres tall.*

*'I'm here. Here. Can't you see me?' Her mother skips by, ignoring Katherine screaming out for her. Her mother keeps skipping as the Beast screams, drowning in water, choking in water, gasping, 'Hiding girl ... hiding girl ... hiding girl.'*

'Please. Please help me,' Katherine murmurs in her sleep, rustling sheets, stretching out her arms.

\* \* \*

'I don't want to go on this harbour cruise. I shouldn't have said yes.' Katherine's voice rises in increasing panic. 'Where's Mum? How do I look?'

'Mum's finishing the washing.' Rachel puts down her magazine. 'How do I know what you look like? I can't see you. Come out of the bedroom and I'll do a few last-minute touches to your make-up.'

'No one can fix me. I can't go. You can't force me to go. Mum can't either.' Katherine flings herself onto her bed, but she leaves her door open, signalling to Rachel that she can come in.

'You're acting odd, Katherine.' Rachel wanders into her sister's room with a comb and some lip gloss. 'That dress is great on you.'

'You can see my burns. My hair doesn't cover my shoulders.' Katherine rolls onto her back, holding her stomach. 'I shouldn't have bought this dress. And I look fat. Fat. Fat.'

'You're a fathead, if you ask me.' Rachel takes her hand, pulling her up. 'And you're wrong, the dress looks just right. I wouldn't say it if I didn't mean it. You're scared, that's all.'

'No, I'm not.'

'Let me fix the braid in your hair. You always let me.'

'Well, I'm not a little girl any more, Rachel. No.'

'You're acting like one.'

Katherine breathes quickly, trying to control her panic. 'All right, if it makes you feel better. And I'm not scared.' She turns away from Rachel to face the open window. The temperatures have been dropping with the cool southerly breezes. Rachel rustles the ends of her sister's hair, then gives her the lip gloss.

Kookaburras. They're perched contentedly on the clothesline, not caring that there is washing to be hung up or drama inside the house. Katherine starts when they suddenly flap into the trees and disturb a plain brown butterfly. Then she notices her mother carrying her wicker basket. Her mother is wearing her washing blouse stained with bleach and scrubbing. It's calming, watching her mother bend to pull sheets and towels from the wicker basket — pegging, bending, pulling, pegging, enjoying the breeze as she completes her familiar cycle. For a moment, her mother stops to watch the butterfly land softly on a white sheet. Katherine watches the butterfly too.

Katherine half listens to Rachel's chatter about her technician's course, her work, and promises that she'll have a great time at the dance. The brown butterfly leaves the white sheet to flitter through the garden of marigolds and sweet-smelling jasmine. *Brown butterfly, brown butterfly, you're protected tonight in my mother's garden. Am I protected too?*

*Swollen eyelids shut tight. Head shaven bare. The woman strokes the baby's face. A seven-year-old girl holds onto the woman's skirt. A plastic tube feeds into the baby's nose and a drip is taped onto her arm. A catheter empties urine into a bag. Her arms are in splints. Her small body wrapped in gauze. Her hands are in mittens also tied to splints. She tries to open her eyes, searching through the swelling.*

*The nurse comes to check tubes and vital signs.*

*The woman brushes back her dark wispy hair and looks up at the nurse. 'What is wrong with that baby? Where is her hair? ... Her face? ... Her body?'*

*'Remember the doctor spoke to you about it?' The nurse's voice gently persists. 'Remember? Remember?'*

*'No. Spoke to me? No.'*

*'About her body, her face.' Pulling a chair close, the nurses sits next to her. 'The baby will ... she will ... look a little different.'*

*The woman stares, confused, at the nurse in her white uniform. 'Where is Katherine? Where is my baby? My little girl?'*

*The nurse answers softly. 'This is Katherine. You can see her.'*

*'But I can't. I can't ... see her. I can't see her.'*


'Katherine, are you ready?' her mother calls as she comes into the house. She stops when she sees her daughter with her long, brown hair flowing and the warmth of black velvet embracing her. 'You look beautiful.'

'That's what mothers are supposed to say.'

'I mean it. You are my beautiful daughter tonight.'

'Come on, Mum.'

Rachel calls. 'Katherine, you'll miss the boat.'

'Is that meant to be a joke? Not very humorous.'

Her mother sits in the front seat beside Rachel. 'I have saved nearly enough for a new car.'

'Don't you like mine, Mum?' asks Rachel. The car starts with only three turns of the ignition. Rachel smirks. 'No one can say that this car isn't the best now, can they?'

'Terrific car,' Katherine calls out from the back seat. 'It's better than no car,' she whispers under her breath.

Rachel drives through dimly lit back streets, over speed humps that make the car sound like it is falling apart, until she reaches their favourite route. Winding alongside the national park, summer has brought colour to the grey-greens of the bush. Red-pronged banksias, soft yellow wattle buds, fluffs of white gum flowers flicker between headlights and the last rays of sun. Katherine watches the eucalyptus trees, vaguely listening to her mother talk to Rachel about a movie they're seeing tonight.

Rachel reaches the freeway. There is no conversation now as she concentrates on joining the stream of cars, turning into the freeway and putting her foot on the accelerator. The radio hums an old Beatles tune as they head for the quay, settling into the rhythm of the car's spinning wheels.

Finally, Rachel pulls up alongside the kerb. 'We're here,' she smiles triumphantly.

'You had better go, Katherine. You must not be late. Do not worry, we will be here at eleven to collect you.'

Katherine slides out of the back seat, stands beside the car, straightens her dress, touches her hair, looks around, waits, straightens her dress again, rubs her hands along her pantyhose, looks around ...

Rachel calls out of the window, 'Are you going or not? We'll be late for the movies, you know.'

'You won't be late. Don't be so mean. I've just got to get my dress straight.'

'It is straight.' Rachel waves her away. 'And I put your camera and some extra lip gloss in your bag. You forgot them.'

'You look lovely. Just go now, Katherine.'

Katherine reluctantly walks across the road towards the promenade, leaving her sister and mother watching her. Street buskers playing guitars, open-air cafes, the lights of the harbour, create an excitement. Katherine shakes her head. *I'm going to have a good time. I am. Damn it, I'm sick of being scared.* Katherine sees her friends at the ticket stand. She takes a deep breath, then runs to join them.

'Hi, everyone. You all look fantastic. Love your bag, Liz.'

'Made from vinyl, not leather.'

'We all love animals, but no lectures today,' Julia interrupts.

'There's William.' Katherine glances at him, then looks away.

'Mr Roberts is over there. He's one of the bouncers tonight.' Liz thinks that's funny.

'He's wearing an earring. Can you believe it?'

'Have you got your camera?'

Their talk moves between dresses and guys and insecurities as the girls board the ferry to meet the guys.

The lights of the city sparkle as the ferry heads out into the harbour. The lights inside the boat are dimmed, the band loud, the dance floor empty as groups of the opposite sex settle into opposing corners of the boat. A few couples edge towards the floor, moving in time with the beat, but they don't dare start dancing. The girls giggle and start to move to the music until one of them pulls another, who pulls another, who pulls another ... who pulls Katherine uncertainly onto the floor, until they're all jumping around, circling, pumping energy. Jessie sees Katherine and joins her on the dance floor, dragging Greg with her. The first male. A sign that the guys in the corners can join the dancing and start partying seriously.

The band takes a break. Girls hang around the drummer and guitarist. A few guys drool around the lead singer, who's wearing a black leather bodysuit and a diamond stud in her nose. The build-up of sweat and body heat from the dance floor eases with the break, as people retreat onto the decks.

'Come on, Katherine. Let's go and fix our make-up.' Jessie looks at Greg. 'Be back soon.' They push their way through the crowds for serious discussion. Jessie can hardly wait until they're in the Ladies. 'He's so nice, Katherine. I know I let you down, but

you'll just have to forgive me, because Greg is ...
I can't explain it. Don't you think he's got the most
gorgeous green eyes. Pale green, so romantic, and he's
so tall. He plays rugby for the A's as well as
basketball. We can go to watch him next Saturday.
He's got some really good-looking friends you might
like. What do you think?'

'I think you've lost it. Your brain, that is.'
Katherine half laughs, *and you don't deserve it, but I
forgive you.*

'Very funny. What do you really think?'

'He seems friendly, but I don't know him yet.'

Other girls move around the mirrors, adjusting
skirts, smoothing on lipstick, combing hair before
they leave the security of closed doors and girlfriends
for another onslaught outside. One girl reports
excitedly, 'Some of the guys have these pewter flasks.
They're drinking on the top deck. Marc's there. Do
you want to go up?'

Katherine bites her lip. *Now I know where not to
go.*

'Who cares about Marc and those losers.' Jessie
checks her make-up in the mirror.

'Not me,' Katherine snaps. She stares at her
reflection in the mirror. *Not me. Not me. Girl who
has to hide. I'm not going to the deck, but not
because of you, Marc. I don't want to hide up there
sneaking sips from a pewter flask. It's pathetic. I
don't care what you think. You're ... unimportant to
my life. Unimportant.* Slowly, she brushes her hair,

careful to camouflage her neck and shoulder. She takes Rachel's lip gloss out and smoothes it over her lips. *This is my night with my friends. They accept me and I am what I am, at least tonight. I've seen a few frogs on the ferry, Marc, and guess what? You're one of them — a big, ugly, croaky toad. I don't like toads.* Katherine smiles. *And you never know, there might even be a prince out there for me.*

Jessie and Katherine go back to the dance floor. Greg's waiting for Jessie. 'Do you want to go onto the deck and see the ocean?' He takes her hand.

Katherine winks. 'There are a lot of stars tonight.' Voices from the dance floor call out for her. 'In a minute, I'm coming.' She fossicks in her bag, takes out a camera. 'One photo. Smile Jessie, Greg.' She leaves them standing together as she moves onto the dance floor, her camera flashing as she takes photos of the band, her friends, some of the guys, a photo of Mr Roberts, who's dancing with the Head of the English Department.

It is late by the time the heat and energy disperse the crowd. A few escape to the cooler air of the decks. Others lean against the bar with its no-alcohol signs or sit at packed tables. Katherine dances next to Julia and Liz until Julia leaves with a lanky, fair-haired guy to get drinks. The music becomes faster and Liz joins a circle of wild ones. Katherine doesn't know how she ends up dancing with William. His movements aren't quite coordinated and he steps out of tune to the drummer's beat. He talks about going north to surf after his exams. *I love the sea.* Then I want to go to university. 'I'd like to do teaching.'

She stares at him for a moment, then bends her head. *You've got hazel eyes. Hazel, like kookaburra feathers.*

They dance and dance, joining Liz's group for a while, separating when he gets her a drink, dancing closely as the music slows, discoing apart when it's wild. The beat is hectic when Mr Roberts bumps into Katherine. 'What noise is this? Ho!'

'Mr Roberts, we're not in English class are we?' Katherine shouts back.

'No, but there are a lot of Romeos and Juliets here.'

'Are we all going to die as star-crossed lovers, Mr Roberts?'

'Don't think so, but I've just broken up a bit of fighting going on between a few "lovers" on the deck.'

'You mean frogs, Mr Roberts?'

'What are you talking about? Anyway, just give me your camera.' He takes it from her and snaps Katherine laughing with Liz, Katherine swinging with the beat, Katherine flashing cheesy grins at Wiilliam. 'Have a great night,' he says, handing back the camera.

*I will, Mr Roberts.* Katherine looks up at William, who is much taller than she is.

Jessie and Greg arrive on the dance floor. Julia comes back and Liz is still unstoppable. William's arms circle Katherine's waist. *I never thought ... William. Am I being ridiculous? It's your eyes. And you love the ocean. You've got really special eyes ... William.* The name circles inside her head as others return for the last songs and the floor is filled with movement and provocative dancing.

The lead singer gyrates to the guitarist's strings, seducing the microphone with her lips against the wire mesh. William swirls Katherine around and around so that black velvet clings to her as the ferry splashes homeward, sliding through the water.

'How was it?' Rachel and her mother ask together.

'The best night. The best.'

*The whirlpool pulls her downwards, pulls her. Then there is a hand. It takes hold of the Beast's hand, dragging her up, but the hand is gentle and she moves easily through the whirlpool, floating upwards with her brown hair softly circling her until she's in his arms. The Prince holds Katherine.*

# CHAPTER SIX

Photomania. Everyone yells, 'Show me. Show me.'

'I look so stupid.' Julia groans.

'You don't. But Mr Roberts does.' Jessie points. 'Just look at him.'

'Oh, there's one of you and Greg.'

Looking over Jessie's shoulder, Liz interrupts. 'William's cute.'

Katherine blushes.

'Are you going to go out with him?' asks Liz.

'Don't be an idiot,' Katherine mutters.

Photos pass under desks, across aisles, through Physics and Maths and Assembly and the last class of the day, English. Mr Roberts lifts up his hands, accepting defeat. 'All right. I don't think we're going to get very far in class today.' He fossicks in his briefcase and produces his own photographs. 'Now you Juliets, I think we'll dedicate this lesson to serious study of the dance.'

There's so much gossip and laughing that when the bell rings no one's in a hurry to leave, except Katherine. She has an appointment in the city at the doctor's. Packing her bag quickly, she leaves Jessie in charge of the photos and any important information Katherine might miss. 'I'll ring you later.'

When Katherine peers through the glass door into the doctor's reception room, she sees her mother waiting patiently next to an artificial palm tree. She forces down irritation as she pushes open the glass door, nods at the receptionist who knows her, then makes her way towards the palm tree. She sits next to her mother. 'You didn't have to come.'

'It was not a problem to leave work early. The manager is very understanding. I will start work early for the shift on Saturday, that is all.'

*I don't want you to begin earlier. You'll have to get up at five in the morning*, Katherine whispers under her breath. 'You don't have to any more.' *It makes me feel rotten and why do you have to any more?* Katherine rustles through a woman's magazine without reading anything. *I'm seventeen, nearly eighteen, for god's sake. I can see the doctor for a checkup without you.*

'Katherine.' The receptionist calls out her name. Her mother and Katherine stand up together and the receptionist smiles. 'You look more like your mother every day, Katherine.'

'Everyone says that.' Katherine glances at her mother with her olive complexion and dark hair. The Professor acknowledges them as they open the surgery door. He's around sixty, with thinning hair and a softly-spoken, slightly nervous tone to his voice, and one of the most eminent surgeons in the country.

He commences the examination, interspersing it with the usual questions. 'How are you?' 'Is there any tightening of skin?' 'Is Biology still your favourite subject?' 'Let me check your range of movement.' 'How's your swimming?' As he raises her right arm, he sees the tear.

Her mother reaches out to touch her daughter. 'Katherine, you did not tell me.'

Katherine jerks away from her touch. 'It's nothing, Mum. And you know I can't have a graft now. Swimming trials are on.' Her voices peters out. *I don't want to explain. Don't make me explain.* Katherine presses her hands against her chest. *I feel like I can't breathe. Give me some room, Mum.*

Her mother protests, but stops when the Professor answers, 'All right. We can leave it for a little while. You know how to keep it clean.'

'I will make sure Katherine looks after herself properly.'

The Professor nods.

*This is humiliating. I don't want the Professor to think I can't look after myself. Mum, I can take care of myself.* The Professor writes notes in a thick folder with red tags jutting out in odd places. Katherine watches his fountain pen scratch black onto white paper, then she looks up at her mother. *Mum, you have to let me grow up. You just have to. I can't be your little girl forever.*

*It is Tuesday morning and her mother drops Rachel at school on her way to Mrs Hampton's. Katherine hasn't started school yet, even though she's six. She loves going with her mother to Mrs Hampton's, but hates the bus trip there. The bus makes her ill. She's never allowed to eat before she rides on the bus because she feels sick. Her mother tells funny jokes and makes her laugh on the trip so that she doesn't think about throwing up.*

*Mrs Hampton lives in a huge house that overlooks Sydney Harbour. Katherine watches the yachts from the balcony. Sometimes Mrs Hampton is there while her mother cleans. She's always kind to Katherine, wanting to give her ice-cream and toys. Katherine accepts the toys, but never the ice-cream.*

*As her mother rubs the windowpanes, making them sparkle, Mrs Hampton walks over. She's hesitant. 'I hope you won't consider me rude ...' Katherine's mother stops rubbing the panes. 'It's just that I've noticed with Katherine ... well ... her hair, her face ... and she's awkward ... can't lift her arm very well ... She can't run properly, can she? Do you ... would you mind taking her to see my doctor?'*

*Her mother looks up at Mrs Hampton. There's a catch in her voice. 'No, I would not mind.' She doesn't tell Mrs Hampton about her many trips to the hospitals. She's gone to so many hospitals in the city, until the doctors won't see her. She doesn't tell her about the pleadings, the arguments, the examinations of Katherine. No one will do anything for her little girl. She overheard them once. 'I don't think she understands English. The girl is all right. It's the mother who needs help.' They call her pushy, neurotic, but she still takes Katherine back to the hospitals. At the hospital Outpatients she speaks in her soft Italian accent to those people standing behind barricades of glass and Laminex. They talk to her slowly, loudly, as if her quiet Italian sounds make her deaf, as if she's ignorant. They tell her 'it's only cosmetic, not covered by the health system ... nothing can be done.'*

*'No, I would not mind taking Katherine to your doctor.'*

*Mrs Hampton rings the surgery then. Makes the appointment for that afternoon. 'Urgent,' she whispers to her family doctor. 'Urgent.'*

*Katherine and her mother wait in reception. When the receptionist calls, her mother takes Katherine's hand and they walk together into the doctor's room. The doctor starts when he sees Katherine. Then he smiles and points to two chairs on the other side of the desk.*

*The mother tells him that Katherine can't stand straight any more, that she sometimes feels sick.*

*'She shouldn't be ill from the scarring. Are you sick Katherine?' he asks gently.*

*She doesn't answer, and holds onto her mother's knitted cream jacket.*

*Her mother takes off her daughter's white top. Katherine's body bends forward, contorting her stomach so that she holds her stomach when she eats. The doctor examines her, tracing his hand down her head, scarred by ridges and burns. Her neck bends towards her right shoulder as if attached to it. She can't straighten fully because scars can't grow or flex like the rest of her. 'I've seen enough.'*

*Katherine's mother presses her hand to her mouth. Slowly she dresses Katherine, then holds her close.*

*'I've never seen anything like this here. A child with this type of scarring. A child who isn't given the chance to grow properly.' He mutters under his breath. 'We have a health system, the expertise ...' Suddenly the doctor is angry. He pulls the phone sharply towards him and calls his friend. A plastic surgeon. 'You have to see this little girl now. She can't pay, but you have to do something. I'm asking a favour. You owe me. We owe this little girl.'*

*There is so much surgery. Six operations. Her mother is there looking after her, feeding, bathing, telling her stories, running home to Rachel, who is looked after by a neighbour, but coming back early for Katherine so that she knows she isn't alone. Her mother leaves her soft, knitted jacket with Katherine when she goes to the toilet or has a break or goes home late in the evening for Rachel, and Katherine cries until she comes back.*

*Staff at the Burn Unit, doctors, the Professor, do favours and start a series of hair transplants. The doctors graft twenty-two centimetres of skin onto Katherine's sides and Katherine can stand straight for the first time in three years. She eats ice-cream.*

*I love you, Mum. You don't know it, but to me you're a saint. Like Joan of Arc. I couldn't have made it without you, but I'm older now. I have to do things myself. Do you understand, Mum? It's taken a long time, but I am grown up.* The Professor examines behind her knees, her right leg, her stomach, chest. The Professor checks Katherine's scalp, most of it covered with her own expanded skin. She has long hair now. He lifts her hair up to examine her head with its misshapen scars.

Katherine shuts her eyes tightly, ignores her mother who is as pale as the painted lilies hanging above her, then she demands, 'I want to wear my hair up.' She takes a breath, opens her eyes. 'I want to look like everyone else.'

Her mother interrupts as if to protect her. 'You do.'

*You're a liar.* 'Mum, please don't.'

The Professor's black-framed degrees stare down at Katherine.

'I don't want to hide scars under my hair. I don't want the side of my face to be like this. You've helped me before, Professor. Please.'

'Katherine, I don't know.' The Professor doodles on his notepad.

'Please. You can help me.'

'I don't know about that.'

\* \* \*

There's tension between Katherine and her mother as they leave the professorial suite. Her mother is angry. 'Why did you not tell me about your arm? You must not swim this year.'

'Mum, I don't want to talk about this. If I swim it's my decision, not yours.' Katherine slams the car door shut. It's the new family car, which her mother bought after taking them to every car yard in the city. Rachel had said that she was happy. 'No more lifts,' but she hadn't meant it and still drives Katherine to the beach for training.

'Please, Katherine. You will destroy our new car. I work hard for this car.'

'I work hard too, Mum.'

'What is wrong with you? You are upsetting me.' Her mother grasps the wheel tightly as she edges out from the kerb. The peak-hour traffic is heavy with cars beeping and petrol fumes seeping into the air.

Katherine shudders. *I can't deal with this.* She turns on the radio. *I don't want to make you angry or upset, Mum, but you make ME angry and upset. I try to do everything you want. I study and help in the house. I'm starting a job as a waitress on Saturday afternoon. I'll pay for myself now. Let me make my own choices. If I decide to swim, then I'll do it. It's my life and I'll live with the consequences.* They're on the freeway now and her mother loosens her grasp on the steering wheel as the traffic flows quickly and smoothly towards the outer suburbs.

'What is this about more surgery, Katherine?'

'I want more done.' *I'm not a little girl any more. I can speak for myself. The way you treated me in front of the Professor was humiliating. How could you? You don't live with scars. I do. I know what it really means, you'll never know. Sometimes I want to hide in a cupboard where it's dark and safe and no one can make me feel ugly. Where I'm invisible. But I don't want to be invisible all my life. I can't live like that.*

*Is that what you want for me, Mum?*

She asks Katherine questions. Katherine answers in monosyllables until her mother is annoyed. 'This is enough. I am tired from work and rushing to get you to the doctor's and I have to cook tonight. Is Jessie coming for dinner?'

'Yes.'

'Is she staying over tonight?'

'Yes.' *Thank god. I can get away from you.*

Her mother presses her lips closely together and focuses on the road. Katherine looks out of the window, waiting for the familiar stretch of eucalyptus trees and wattle blossoms. They're silent until they reach home.

Rachel is cooking. 'Thought I'd save you the trouble, Mum. Stir-fry chicken in my special sauce. Sounds good? By the way, Jessie's here already.'

'Thank you, Rachel. There are some mangoes, Kiwi fruit and oranges in the fridge. I will make fruit salad. It will cool us all down. Hello, Jessie. How are your parents?'

'Good, thanks.'

Jessie and Katherine disappear into Katherine's bedroom. The *Romeo and Juliet* soundtrack hums under the door as Katherine closes it against her mother. She shakes her mother from her mind. *I'm so glad you're here, Jessie. I just want to forget about this afternoon.*

Jessie is lounging on the bed. 'I like that song even though it has THE DREADED TITLE.' She sings with the music.

'Well, tell me about him,' Katherine says as she changes into her blue top and denim jeans.

'About who?' Jessie smiles.

'As if you don't know.'

'Do you mean Greg?'

'Who else? Or are you seeing another man?'

'Never!' Jessie dramatically presses her hands against her heart.

Katherine shakes her head. 'You're definitely an actor, Jessie. Forget Physics.'

'You know I'd never give up Physics. Anyway, Greg is picking us up about seven tonight for the play. I can't wait to see Greg. The more I see him, the cuter he gets. I like his red hair and I like him.' She hugs Katherine's pillow. 'It'll be a great night. The play should be good. Better than reading it in class.'

'I don't mind reading the play. You can stop when you want. Re-read parts. Get coffee in the middle of a scene. Think about what's happening.'

'It's because you like Mr Roberts.'

'I don't think so.'

'Sorry, it's William now, isn't it.'

Katherine grabs the pillow from under Jessie's head, then throws it at her.

Jessie flings it back. She's laughing. 'I can't help teasing you.'

'It's not very funny.'

'Sorry.' Jessie sits up. 'Thanks a lot for letting me stay tonight. I really mean that. Dad would give me a hard time if he knew I was going to the play with Greg. I'm supposed to concentrate on studies, not him.'

'Your dad's looking out for you, that's all. You want to get into Physics and it's really difficult.'

'Come on. That doesn't mean I can't go out with Greg. Life isn't just studying, is it?'

'No. I still think you're lucky to have a dad.'

'You don't know anything about it. Can we not talk about this tonight? I want to have a good time. Greg's a much better topic.'

'Sure.' Katherine nods.

The words from the *Romeo and Juliet* soundtrack make Jessie take a slow breath. 'That's so romantic.'

Katherine smiles. 'So how serious are you really about Greg?' *William hasn't even rung me. He probably never will. Why should he?*

'Serious, I guess.' Jessie looks around the room. 'It's a mess in here, Katherine.'

'I've heard that before. Come on, tell me.'

'I don't know how to explain it, but when Greg's with me I feel special. I love him stroking my hair. It makes me shiver. I just want to touch him and when he touches me … it's … special.' Jessie wraps her arms around herself.

*Shiver? Touched? What's that? Not Mama holding me. Not Rachel taking my arm. Not the Professor examining my grafts. Special? Will someone ever want to touch me like that? I don't think it'll ever happen to me.* Katherine runs her hand along the back of her neck. 'Have you …?'

'I've done some things, more than kissing, but not too much. Greg wants to, but no. Not yet. If Dad thought I'd done anything, he'd kill me.' Jessie rolls her eyes. 'If you ask me, he's thinking about all those girlfriends he had before Mum. I think he married Mum because she wouldn't go to bed with him. Imagine being so stupid to marry someone for sex?'

*Sex? Someone touching my scars, feeling my arms, stroking my back, shoulders, the roughness along my neck and under my hair … seeing me.* Katherine shudders. *I'd be afraid he'd hate me.*

Jessie lies back on the bed. 'It feels safe when Greg holds my hand. That's stupid, I know, but I get this funny, warm feeling inside me.'

Katherine shakes her head. *I can't even imagine someone wanting me. Men? I don't know who they are. I was a baby when my father left. There's just Mum, Rachel, me. No one has even asked me out, and what would I do if someone did? William danced with me. He put his arms around me. Did I feel safe?*

'Let's play *Romeo and Juliet* again.'

'I'd like to feel safe, Jessie.' Katherine hesitates. 'You know, after my burns, my father left.'

Jessie nods. 'I know.'

'Rachel hates him. I don't understand what I feel about him.' Katherine touches the roughness along her arms. 'After the burns, he came around a few times, and that was it. Never saw him again. How could he just leave?'

Jessie shrugs. 'It's wrong, but I guess some men are like that.'

'He sends us birthday cards.' *I don't want to talk about him. Why am I?* 'Rachel's got his red hair and freckles. I'm glad I look like Mum. He's never helped us. You'd think he would have.' Katherine stops abruptly.

'You don't need him, Katherine.'

'Maybe you're right.'

Katherine's relieved when Rachel calls them for dinner. The chicken is spicy, a mix of basil and chilli. Everyone has to drink jugs of water. The fruit salad is cool and the sweet, yellow flesh of the mango takes the bite out of the red chilli.

'Sorry, Mum, about being in a bad mood before.' *I love you. Where would I be without you?* Katherine gets up from the table and starts clearing the dishes.

The doorbell rings. Greg. There are embarrassed 'hellos' and the usual talk.

'Don't worry about the dishes.' 'Are you looking forward to seeing the play?' 'When will you be home?' 'Have a good time.' 'Drive carefully.'

They escape through the front door.

# CHAPTER SEVEN

Katherine speaks to the coach about swimming for the regionals one day and maybe even the nationals. He wants to talk to her about it after the trials. 'I'll see how well you do and how serious you are.'

Swimming training is five mornings a week before school. Then there is the gym and push-ups and strengthening exercises. Katherine likes running in the evening, after studying, when it's cooler. She always runs the same route down along the ghost gum track, startling rabbits when she whistles to the grey and pink galahs perched on high branches.

Sometimes Katherine has to miss training. Sometimes she doesn't go to the gym, but she always runs. 'You won't be a winner if you're not totally committed,' the coach shouts. He concentrates on other swimmers who never miss training. They miss school instead. They don't have a weekend job, doctors' appointments, shopping trips into the city.

She doesn't argue with the coach, but he shakes her purpose. *Committed. Am I?* Katherine's tear doesn't heal even though she's careful to treat it properly. She won't let her mother see it and they fight until her mother shouts at her and Katherine slams her bedroom door.

On Saturday, she argues as usual with Rachel over the mess Katherine has left in the bathroom, studies two hours of Maths, goes to the gym, and rings Jessie, who seems to have endless things to say about Greg. 'He's the most interesting guy in the world,' Katherine jokes. Then it's Saturday afternoon. The cafe. Financial independence.

Katherine has to wear black trousers and a white T-shirt. She likes the uniform because it gives her protection from the curiosity of people who pretend not to look at the scarring of her arms and legs. The manager doesn't mind that she wears her hair out.

The cafe isn't too busy. Two ladies sit eating salad sandwiches on wholemeal bread. A man in the corner reads his newspaper and sips a cappuccino. There are three tables outside with four director's chairs at each of them. Katherine goes to the back of the cafe, says hello to the cook, then puts on a black apron and starts wiping down benches in time with the music playing on the radio. She's staring out of the window when a crowd of people sit down at the outside tables. She has already discovered that's the way it is in a cafe. Flood or famine. Katherine gets the menus and as she hands them out she sees him. Marc.

'Didn't know you worked here,' Marc says casually.

*Don't blush, Katherine, don't dare,* but she feels her face getting hot. 'Started last week. This is my second Saturday.'

They order burgers, colas, make lots of jokes. 'We're going to the beach. I do surfboat rowing for the lifesaving club.' He stammers a little. 'I hear you're a good swimmer. You'd like surf sports.'

*Are you trying to be nice? Is that you, Marc?* 'I can swim.'

Katherine doesn't wait for a response, escaping into the cafe and only coming out to clear dishes. When she leaves the bill on the table, Marc looks at her as if he wants to say something. He doesn't. There is a tip for Katherine. She watches them disappear around the corner. *That was awful, Marc. Hope you don't come back again.*

It is the regional clubs' swimming meet. Jessie's going to be there for the big event. Rachel insists on driving her beat-up car, not her mother's new Ford. 'My car deserves to be there after all those times she's driven Katherine to training.'

'Is it a person?' Katherine laughs.

'Well, nearly.'

The southerly wind whips up the surf, which pounds against the beach sand. The sea water of the pool ripples as if in anticipation. There are crowds, coaches, swimmers, local newspapers, excitement. The microphone blares for competitors to get ready. Freestyle, backstroke, breaststroke, butterfly, relays, medleys. 100 metres, 200 metres, 400 metres, 800 metres. Heats. Heats. Semi-Finals.

Finals. Eight swimmers. Katherine's rubber cap adheres like glue. Synthetic nylon moulds onto her body so there's no definition between body, costume, costume, body. No friction; fast. Eight pairs of legs on starting blocks. Katherine looks out to the sea, then bends forward. Waiting. Waiting. Katherine sees only blue expanding into the horizon. She does not see her mother in the stands, her sister's banner, Jessie waving, the coach's raised fists. There is only Katherine, the water, the horizon ... the gun.

The coach roars from the side of the pool as Katherine sucks in air hard, blowing out air hard. Her arms strain, edging against seconds that tick like a bomb in her head. Tick. Tick. Faster. Extra effort. More effort. More.

One. Two. They pass her. *I have to get there first. Faster, Katherine, faster.* Catch up. Her team-mate is number three. Four passes her. The swimmers' wake forces water against her face until she can't see the horizon. Too many swimmers in front. Slower. Her arms ache. Crowds shout for the winners — first, second, third place. Splashing. Number five touches the wall. Katherine is number six. She pulls off her cap, dives under the water, re-emerging with her hair smooth against her head.

She nods at the coach and her team-mates and her mother, but she can't hear them, see them. She climbs the rough iron ladder out of the pool, heading for the athletes' area. The dressing room is splintered with talking and changing and preparing for other races. She locks herself into a shower cubicle. Turns on the water. Quiet. *Sixth*. Only the running of water down her face, her breasts, her back, splashing against white tiles, swirling down the corroded iron drain. *Sixth. Is this it?*

'To reach the final is terrific,' Jessie congratulates her.

Katherine listens as her mother and Jessie talk at her about the race and swimming. Rachel looks at her sister. 'It's okay, Katherine.'

Rachel changes the subject. 'Does anyone want some gum?'

Jessie takes a piece.

Katherine shakes her head. 'No, thanks.' She turns away.

The final race is swum. The coach meets his swimmers for a postmortem, with congratulations for some, a rallying of spirits for others, offers for others, training for everyone. As Katherine wraps her towel around herself and turns to walk off with some of her team-mates, the coach calls her over. 'I know how you can lose extra seconds off your time, Katherine.'

As always, she hides inside the protection of her towel. She presses an edge of the towel under her arm. Surprising herself, she answers, 'I'm not fast enough.' *That's the truth. The truth.* Katherine looks away from the coach. A surfboat smashes against the waves, oars paddling furiously, being thrown up, half jutting into space, crashing into troughs, lurching, spiraling, winning against the sea.

'Just surfers. Would you listen, Katherine.' The coach shakes his head. 'If you want it enough, you can be faster.'

'I came sixth.' *Do I feel all right about that? Maybe. I made the finals. That's an achievement. I'm just not as fast, as committed as the others. Can I accept that?*

'You're fast.'

'Not fast enough.' *What's this about? I've never been your star swimmer anyway.*

'You'd have to train harder than you are doing now. It's tough but you could swim for the nationals, maybe even Australia.'

Katherine shakes her head.

'I'd like you to apply for entry into ...' the coach hesitates a little, 'the Paralympic Games.'

She looks confused, remembering wheelchairs and crutches. After training sessions, she'd say hello to them in the changing rooms and they'd say hello back to her.

'If you get in, you'd win the one hundred metre and two hundred metre freestyle, and maybe others.'

Katherine observes the black stopwatch the coach holds in his rough hands. Too much sun has freckled his arms, blotching blondish hair and brown spots right up to his elbows. *I don't like your hands, Coach.* Her eyes dart to his face, to the watch, back to his face. *I don't like you.*

'Australia's the leading country for those games. You'd win gold. I know it.'

*Gold? Winning? Is that what winning is? I don't like you, Coach.* She runs her fingers under her hair, touching the side of her face. 'But those athletes are in wheelchairs or blind or ...' *Am I the same? Am I?*

'I think you could qualify.'

'Qualify?' She runs her fingers over the scars on her thigh. *Is that what you see when I'm on the starting block? When my arms are stretching through the water, is that what you see? Scars?* Suddenly panic grips her stomach and she bends forward. *Mama help me. I'm scared.* She repeats in confusion, 'Qualify?' *Rachel, there's a man here calling me Mud Face, Frankenstein, Pineapple. Am I so different?*

'I want you to seriously think about it.'

The night is warm but Katherine shivers. She looks up at the coach. *I don't like you, Coach.* 'I feel like it'd be cheating.' *I think I hate you, Coach.*

*The school is a brown brick two-storey building with steps disappearing into corridors and closed doors. Children fly down the steps like bees on a mission from their hive. They stop to stare at Katherine, who holds onto her mother's skirt. They flap and flutter before they continue their flight onto the green playing fields or the canteen line.*

*Her mother is wearing her cream jacket, knitted by Nonna. Katherine loves that jacket and when terrible monsters frighten her in the night, her mother gives it to her. In the morning the jacket is crushed and warm. Her mother irons it then.*

*They have an appointment with the Principal. The secretary tells them to wait. Katherine wanders around the room, investigating timetables pinned on a board and a lime-green playing block that is stuck under a bookcase.*

*The secretary tells Katherine's mother that they can go into the office. The Principal stands when they enter. Motioning to two brown vinyl chairs, he stiffly introduces himself before sitting down in his swivel chair. He bends forward, resting his hands on the brown wooden desk. Protected by a computer, a stack of multicoloured files, a phone and the paraphernalia of his job, he starts: 'I have discussed Katherine with the Education Department.' He presses his hands together. 'She's an unusual case. We haven't the back-up staff to really cater for her special needs.'*

*'What do you mean?' Her mother takes Katherine's hand.*

*'Well, she's got ... how can I explain? You understand.'*

*'No, I do not understand.' She strokes Katherine's head and Katherine smiles.*

'She's not quite ... Her movement is restricted. She can't play like the other children, can she?'

'That is untrue.'

'There needs to be a special education teacher allocated to help her with her work.' He fidgets. 'With her writing at least.'

'Katherine can write her name already and a lot of other things. In two languages, she can write.' She turns to her daughter. 'Come here, Katherine. Show the man that you can write in English and Italian.'

'No, please don't. I'm sorry, but this is really getting us nowhere.' He clears his throat. 'We have no facilities for disabled children.'

Her mother leaves, confused, holding Katherine's hand tightly. She walks past the secretary without acknowledging her, through the corridors, down the steps, past the children flying back into their hive, over the grassy playing fields to the yellow-posted bus stop.

'Am I going to Rachel's school, Mama?'

'We will see.'

There are phone calls and meetings and letters. Community Services say, 'No, your daughter isn't disabled. No, she doesn't qualify for any assistance. No, there is no disability allowance. Yes, you should enrol her in a local school.'

The Education Department says, 'No, your daughter is disabled. She can't go to a local school unless a principal agrees.'

Katherine says, 'You read to me, Mama.' 'Rachel, you play ball with me.' 'I don't like them. They're staring at me.' 'Am I going to school?'

The principals say, 'No.'

But then there is one principal who hesitates, listens. She says she'd like to meet Katherine.

With both Rachel and Katherine beside her, their mother stands outside the principal's office. 'Come in.' The principal catches her breath for a moment when she sees Katherine with her head exposed, unprotected by hair. 'How nice to have you girls visit.' She hands Rachel and Katherine a picture book. Rachel, who is ten, sits on a mat in the corner and reads to her sister the story of how the kangaroo found his tail. Katherine points to the drawings in the book, raising her hand. But she can only reach halfway. She giggles with her sister at the pictures of cheeky possums and wise old owls. The principal watches the girls for a while. Then she turns to ask their mother about Katherine.

'Yes, Katherine does fall over sometimes. Yes, it is hard for Katherine to stretch her arm fully, to run as fast as the others. Yes, Katherine becomes upset sometimes, but Katherine tries everything. She is a happy girl. Katherine is happy even though she has been through so much. Katherine wants to learn, to go to school. You will like Katherine. You will like her. You will.'

'I'm sure I will.' The principal asks the secretary to bring them coffee. The girls don't notice that their *mother is quietly crying and that the principal has her arm around her.*

*Rachel leaves her old school. She's sad to say goodbye to her friends, but there'll be other friends at the new school and there is Katherine to look after.*

*The three of them wait at the bus stop. Katherine and Rachel are wearing the new school uniforms their mother bought them from the secondhand shop. Katherine loves the neatly ironed blue-checked dress that smells of soap and lavender but Rachel isn't so sure. She misses her old grey skirt and white blouse.*

*Katherine is holding her mother's hand tightly when they see the bus come around the corner. Their mother bends to kiss Rachel, then Katherine. 'You girls be good at the new school,' she says as she gently pushes Katherine towards the bus.*

*Rachel takes her sister's hand. 'We're always good, Mama.'*

*'I know you are.' Their mother's voice quivers.*

*She waves as her girls climb the bus steps together. They wave back from their seat. Katherine presses her nose against the pane, making it flat.*

*'I love you,' she whispers.*

# CHAPTER EIGHT

Nonna and Grandpapa are coming out to Australia for Christmas.' *I know, Mum. You've told us ten times already. And it is not until the end of the year.* 'It will be different to their Italian Christmas for them but we will have good food and be together. I have to arrange holidays from my job because everyone wants the holidays then. The garden will need some work. Nonna is a great gardener. Katherine, you will have to move in with Rachel.' Rachel stacks the dishes while her mother wipes down the kitchen bench. Her mother reminisces about eating crusty panini on the rocky seawall with her grown-up brother, visiting the big city of Genoa with its parks and palaces, playing with her cousins among the fishing nets. 'Grandpapa loves the sea and the turquoise water and fishing boats. He will love the harbour of Sydney too.' She laughs like a girl. 'Your Nonna was so angry when Grandpapa would disappear. Where do you think he went?' She doesn't wait for Katherine's answer. 'To his favourite place, looking from the cliffs out over the sea.' She catches her breath. 'He would take me with him sometimes.'

'You miss it, don't you?'

She brushes back her hair lightly. 'Yes, but Australia is home. I could not go back.' Every week for as long as Katherine can remember, there has been a phone call from Italy. Now that her mother is working full-time, she phones them as well.

*Imagine leaving home at nineteen, all by yourself, for a man on the other side of the world. A man you really didn't know, who visited with his backpack and a promise of freedom.*

*Their mother is always telling them that there is no hurry to marry, that sex is dangerous and they have to have careers and a life without men. 'I married your father against my parents' wishes. Grandpapa was strict. He loved his church and the family meals and wanted me to marry one day a boy from our way of life.'*

*'But you ran away with our father.'*

*'Yes, and I broke my parents' hearts.'*

*'And he left you and us.'*

*'Yes.'*

*'Was it worth it, Mum?'*

*She strokes her younger daughter's face gently.*
*'You and Rachel are worth it.'*

'Look, we've got company, Mum.' Katherine goes to the back door to watch the red-blue rosellas pecking at seeds on the grass. With their bright colours and cheeky parrot beaks, they always seem like they are partying.

'I must go to the garden. See, there are weeds.' As their mother starts to walk to the laundry for her gardening tools, she turns to Katherine. 'Have you made an appointment with the Professor to look at your arm yet?'

*Don't ruin things Mum. Don't.* Katherine looks at her hands, trying to control her irritation. *I can't stand you always checking, arranging things for me. I love you, but you have to stop controlling me.* 'I'm seeing the Professor next week.'

'Make sure you tell me when the appointment is.' Her mother takes her spade and goes into the backyard. The rosellas flap a little as she disturbs them, then they return to their pecking.

Katherine shakes her head. She switches on the kettle, gets two mugs, heaps a teaspoon of coffee into each, takes milk from the fridge, and waits for the kettle to boil. Calming down, she watches her mother bend over the garden beds, turning the bush soil that's been fertilised so that soft-petalled roses can grow. A golden butterfly flits past her.

'Coffee,' Katherine announces as she enters Rachel's room. Music plays quietly on her sister's CD deck. Teeth are neatly lined on a shelf. Stacked next to them are some magazines. A vase of jasmine splashes perfume through the room. Rachel is sitting at her desk studying for her exams. Katherine hands her a mug. 'It's got marshmallows in it.'

'Thanks. I'm glad the weather's not so hot any more. I can stand hot coffee again. Great. Marshmallows.' She spoons out a sticky lump. 'You were terrific at the swimming meet.'

'Sure.' A wispy breeze makes the pale blue curtains flutter. 'Mum's happy about the grandparents coming. It'll be strange having them here, especially Grandpapa.'

Rachel talks about that Christmas they spent in Italy until Katherine interrupts.

'I want to ask you something.' Katherine places her mug carefully onto a small table, then sits on the floor. There are no books or tapes or clothes scattered everywhere like in her room. She runs one hand over the thick aqua carpet. 'I've been … reconsidering … swimming. I'm glad I got to the finals. You've been great driving me to training and being at the meets.' She waits. 'I thought about this all last night. Didn't sleep much. But I know something now. I'm as fast as I'll ever be.' Katherine presses her hands into the carpet so that the pile sticks out through her fingers. 'It's my scars … I'm fighting against my own skin.'

Silently, they look at each other.

'The coach said something that's forced me to face who I am. I need to talk about it.' The words come disjointedly like when she was very little, before the climbing bar fall.

'What is it?' Rachel puts her mug down on her desk.

Breathing deeply, Katherine speaks quietly as if still working out her thoughts. 'It seems wrong. The coach said I'd win. That I should swim in the Paralympics ... Am I that? Is that me?' She raises her right arm. The early years of wearing the elastic burn suit over her small body, the creams, the grafts, haven't taken away the scars of third degree burns.

'You got to the finals. I could never do that.'

Katherine's breathing is easier, more regular. 'I don't want to swim any more competitions. It's not that I'm disappointed. Well, I am. I've worked hard for it but the coach forced me to look at myself. I'm different to the rest of the squad.'

'Katherine, you're more than them.'

'I just can't swim for my team any more, or any team.'

Rachel nods.

They listen to the music for a while. Katherine gets up and pretends to flick through the magazines on her sister's shelf. 'Maybe I'll do something with the surf club. Lifesaving? They're always looking for new members and it'd feel good to do something worthwhile, not just for myself.'

Rachel nods again. 'You'll be terrific at it.'

'I don't know.'

'Come on, Katherine. You've already proved you're a champion. Forget about the coach.'

'Easy for you to forget.'

'That was unfair.'

'I suppose so.' Katherine presses her hands against the shelf. 'You're right. Who cares about the coach?'

'No one.'

'No one.' Katherine repeats Rachel's words uncertainly.

'Come on. You'll be doing something new. It'll be great.' Rachel smiles. 'More importantly, I need to know who's driving you to lifesaving training?'

Half smiling, Katherine answers. 'That is important. You're driving me but it won't be at five in the morning.'

'Do you mean earlier?'

'Very funny, Rachel.'

'Lifesaving sounds great.'

'Maybe. I'll have to get the graft done under my arm first. Mum's been bothering me about it.'

'You have to get that done anyway.'

Katherine touches the right side of her face. 'When I see the Professor I'm going to ask him about this.' She lifts up her hair, exposing scars. The skin is tight, pulling at her face, shoulder and neck, rippling under her hair. 'Do you think he can do something?'

'I don't know. Maybe. I'm sure if he can, he will.' Rachel stares at her exam notes, then picks up the coffee mugs to take them to the kitchen. 'I'll make some more coffee with marshmallows. They're not very fattening. I hear if you melt them all the kilojoules escape.'

'Sure.' Katherine suddenly jumps up and disappears out of the room. She's hiding a smile when she reappears.

'Your coffee is over there, Katherine.'

'Do you remember this?'

Rachel laughs. 'Of course. How can anyone forget that?'

Katherine sticks the piece of artificial skin and hair onto her arm. 'The glue isn't great. Look, Rachel.' She puts her arm next to her sister's head. 'No one can call me bald with this on, can they? Hairy days ahead.'

'That's the dumbest joke.'

Katherine strokes the hairy scalp. 'What about making some more braid? You could plait my arm.'

'Don't! You're a nut. I'll drop my coffee.'

'Do you remember that afternoon in the city, when it fell off my head?'

'Katherine, I could hardly forget it. Jessie couldn't stop laughing, especially when she asked that old man if he'd seen a scalp lying around the street. He must have thought she was an axe murderer who sliced off parts of people's bodies. Everyone was looking for that stupid thing. You were so bad when you asked that policeman for help.'

'Well, it cost Mum a lot of money to get it made. Just feel that rubber and look the colour of the hair. Very natural. It's a top-of-the-range scalp. Except it kept falling off. It looks good on my arm, don't you think?'

'If you're a gorilla, Katherine.' Rachel laughs. 'Where *did* we find it after all that?'

'It was the policeman. Remember? The scalp was in the gutter.' Katherine strokes the scalp again. 'Come on, scalp. Let's change the CD to *Romeo and Juliet*. We'll be at the cutting edge of music.'

'Cutting? Your jokes are getting worse.'

Katherine detaches the scalp from her arm and puts it next to the CD.

Shaking her head, Rachel goes back to her dental notes.

'I've got to study too.' Katherine slumps onto the carpet, next to her sister. She opens her Shakespeare and reads, 'Love give me strength, and strength shall help afford.' She looks across at Rachel and asks seriously, 'What do you believe love is?'

'Us, Katherine.'

They smile at each other.

When the phone rings, Katherine's engrossed with the passions of Romeo and Juliet's undying love.

'Do you want to get it?' Rachel asks.

There's no answer.

'Are you deaf or something?' Rachel shakes her head, picking up the phone. 'Katherine. For you. William.'

Katherine throws down her book.

'Oh, I see you're not deaf.' Rachel puts her hand over the mouthpiece. 'By the way, who is William?'

Katherine jumps up. 'Tell you later.' Dragging the line into her bedroom, she closes the door, shoves books aside, sits on the floor with her back against the wall. *Okay, it's probably nothing. He just wants to catch up. I saw him at the bus stop the other day. He probably saw me too.* 'Hi, William.'

'Hi, Katherine. I had a good time at the dance. Did you?'

'Yes.' *Why didn't you ring before? I've been waiting. I thought you didn't like me.*

'I was meaning to call, but I had assignments to finish and I had the basketball competition. I'm in the B's. We got to the semi-finals.'

'I'm starting surf-lifesaving.'

'Sounds great.'

The conversation jerks awkwardly between surfing, hockey and basketball, gradually flowing into school subjects, teachers, friends in common, the latest films. *Are we going to talk forever? Are you going to ask me out? Please ask me out.* 'Well, I've got to go, William.'

'Me too.' There's a pause. 'Do you want to go to the movies?' There's another pause. 'Maybe with a few friends?'

*He's asked me. He's asked me.* 'Sure. I can talk to Jessie and Greg.' *Get a date. A time.* 'When?'

'Is Saturday night okay? Say I pick you up about seven?'

*No. No. Think quick. I don't want Mum to give me a lecture about going out.* 'Can I meet you at the cafe where I work? On High Street. I finish at six.'

'Fine. See you Saturday then.'

Slamming done the phone, Katherine runs into her sister's room. 'Rachel, Rachel. Guess what? Guess. William asked me out, on Saturday. My first Saturday night date.' Then it's all out. 'He's tall, slim but not skinny. I think he's strong, really straight white teeth, except he's got a yellow front tooth, that doesn't matter, it makes him interesting, a surfer, he's in his last year, do you think he likes me?'

CHAPTER NINE

Mr Roberts' English class is the final one on *Romeo and Juliet*. 'Did you enjoy the theatre production?' he asks them all.

'It was great, Mr Roberts. The play made me feel what it was like for Romeo and Juliet. Being in love like that,' Julia answers.

'"Good night, good night! Parting is such sweet sorrow, That I shall say good night till it be morrow." But love isn't so easy, is it? Why?' Mr Roberts points to Jessie.

'I guess there are parents to consider. Romeo's and Juliet's families hate each other. It made it pretty difficult for them.'

Mr Roberts recites the last lines of the play. '"For never was a story of more woe, Than this of Juliet and her Romeo." In the end they both die.'

'But it was illogical. Fate doomed them. I don't believe in that,' Liz calls out.

'So can you control everything? Are some things predetermined?' Mr Roberts strides up the aisle.

Katherine raises her hand. 'Some things you can't change, like who you're born to. Romeo and Juliet came from rich and powerful families. That was good fate. Their families hated each other and that was bad fate.' Katherine hesitates. 'They did the rest themselves.'

Julia interrupts. 'That's a bit tough. Do you think it's their fault that they died?'

'They didn't have to die. They had choice.' Katherine unconsciously presses her hand against her neck. *Choice. You don't understand, Julia.* She looks curiously at her friend. *You haven't been there. How could you know anything? I've got burns that go so deep, I can't feel my body in places. I've got scars. Scars that make people move away from me, or feel sorry for me, or ... I don't know, treat me differently. I have to choose all the time, every day ... Choose to be like my body ... tight, choking, tearing when I reach out ...* Katherine digs her fingernails into the desk. *I have to choose to stay burnt or not. But I'm not burnt inside. I'm perfect inside. Can't you see I'm perfect inside?*

Katherine turns away from the classroom and looks out of the window. There is a huge Port Jackson fig tree spreading shade across the bitumen. *I don't like bitumen. I want to kick it sometimes.*

*I just want to kick things. The pit, my father, Jessie's pretty hair, Rachel, even Mum. I don't like being burnt. Fate? I didn't ask for this. I don't want my scars.* Katherine pinches the roughness of her thigh until Mr Roberts disturbs her thoughts. He is calling out to the class to pay attention. There is an essay he is setting. Katherine forces herself to look away from the bitumen, along the thick knotty roots of the Port Jackson, up the rugged trunk sprouting branches and green leaves. She grits her teeth. *You're breaking up the bitumen, aren't you, fig tree? You're a big, old fighter. Me too. Guess what, Port Jackson fig tree? I'm not going to be stuck with third degree burns forever.*

'The essay topic is: Do the lovers control their destiny?'

*Yes, Mr Roberts. Yes. Yes.*

'Love and Destiny is a great topic to begin with.'

*You're right, Mr Roberts but 'Love and Life' is even better.*

Mr Roberts smiles as he collects his books. 'I saw a few starstruck lovers at the last dance.'

'Me too,' Katherine says under her breath.

'I hope Greg and I don't have the same end as Romeo and Juliet,' whispers Jessie.

'I doubt it.' Katherine is quiet for a moment. *Love and life. No, love of life. That's what I'm choosing.* She asks. 'Can you and Greg come to the movies on Saturday?'

'To see what?'

'Doesn't matter. Anything.' She bends her head. 'William is taking me.'

Jessie gives a scream, making Katherine smile. *Love of life.*

'Fantastic! Terrific! So tell me everything, Katherine. Everything.'

'Marc came into the cafe. I'll tell you about that later, but about William . . .'

'So I'll do the graft for your arm in two weeks.' The Professor writes his notes. He phones through to his secretary to arrange for the hospital admission, then he gives his attention to Katherine and her mother. He speaks carefully. 'Your hair from the extended skin transplants covers the scarring on your neck and head and the right side of your face. There has been a lot of work already done. Further reconstruction is difficult and only succeeds to a point. It may not be successful.'

Katherine studies the framed charts hanging on the surgery walls: colour diagrams of facial and limb reconstructions, circulatory responses in burns patients, variations of epidermis thickness. Then she looks at the Professor. *You can do it.*

'However there is a procedure that I've been developing.' The Professor's white eyebrows edge together. 'It's painful and may not produce the results you want. Do you realise that?'

Katherine nods. *You can do it. I just know it.* Her mother presses her daughter's hand.

Methodically, the Professor explains. 'I would have to graft new skin and tissue onto your shoulder, neck and face in separate operations. You already understand grafting and that it fails sometimes. The blood supply may not develop sufficiently to sustain the grafts. Even if grafting is successful, grafts often may not look like what you want. There would have to be further surgery, especially to define and reshape.' He opens his hands in a gesture of concern. 'I want you both to think about it, talk about it. I'm prepared to go ahead but only if you understand that it may be a disappointment. For now, let's wait until after this graft, then we can discuss it further.'

They leave. Katherine races to catch the lift in the corridor. She holds open the heavy metal doors for her mother. The doors close. It's stuffy inside the lift, which is going up before it does down. Shiny stainless steel and panelled mirrors reflect an anxious fortyish woman with her dark hair in a loose bun, wearing a skirt and cream jacket, and a young woman in jeans and a black T-shirt with her hair hanging loosely around her face.

'Mum, I have to have more surgery done. I have to have it.' Katherine puts the palm of her hand against her face.

'The Professor has always been kind. He never treated me differently because I spoke with an accent. He always explains what is to happen.' Looking at her daughter, she says quietly, 'It will be painful, Katherine. You may be disappointed.' She rubs her forehead with an embroidered handkerchief. 'It is hot in here.'

*It's hot inside. The room is unbearable. Temperatures are raised because Katherine's cold, so cold.*

*Scrub suits, caps, masks, plastic aprons, people in the room smelling of iodine and soap. Gloved hands immerse Katherine in the hydrotherapy tank. Strangers' hands and Mama's hands.*

*Katherine whimpers as the warm water is sponged over her wounds. The narcotics dull her movements as she tries to reach for her mother.*

*'Katherine, you are such a good baby. You are so good and pretty. You have to be really brave because it will be over soon. Over soon.' Her mother starts to sing softly to her, but she stops when she sees the nurse coming with her scissors and forceps. Humming, she strokes Katherine's hand.*

*Blisters opened. Dying tissue stripped away. The smell of decay. Bleeding. Stinging cream. Katherine screaming. Screaming as only a baby can scream. Her mother hovering over her child, sobbing with her baby's sobs.*

The lift opens. The modern glass foyer is busy with people moving between consulting rooms, pathology collections, administration.

'It'll work. Please, Mum.'

Her mother sighs as she steps onto the bitumen footpath. Plain, black, useful bitumen. She turns her back on the glasshouse of busyness and looks at her daughter. 'Yes, if that is what you really want.'

'I do, Mum. I do.'

Saturday afternoon. Rachel has made a black and silver hair ribbon for Katherine.

'What are you wearing for the BIG date?'

'Just my black work pants and my favourite green top.' Katherine grabs her small, stuffed sheepdog. 'Hey, what do you think, Pup? Will my green top bring me luck? What do you think?'

Rachel laughs. 'Pup says you don't need luck. Hold still, so I can put this through your hair.' She carefully loops it into a knot. 'Have you told Mum?'

'Sort of. She knows I'm going to the movies with Jessie and some other friends. I'm not telling her about William yet. I might hate him, so why go through all the boring lectures like "men only want one thing", "they drink too much", "study is more important than men", "you'll have plenty of time afterwards". For god's sake, I'm seventeen and never been kissed. Except by Pup.' She looks seriously into Pup's brown marble eyes. 'And I made the first move, didn't I, Pup? I don't want you to be the only man in my life. Can you cope with that?'

'You're a nut. I'm finished. Come on then, I'm driving you to the cafe today. It's on my way. I've got a dental association meeting tonight.'

Katherine throws Pup onto her bed. 'Don't worry, Pup, I'll tell you all about what happens tonight.

Hope you don't mind, but we'll just be friends from now on. Is that all right?' She puts her top in her bag. 'Let's go.'

Their mother is preparing some dips. Two of her girlfriends are coming over.

'We're leaving now, Mum.'

'Please be home by midnight, both of you. I will wait up.'

'I'll be back by nine.' Rachel rattles her keys.

'You don't have to stay up for me.' Katherine's voice is edgy.

'Let's go.' Rachel grabs her sister's arm.

They drive along the familiar streets of suburbia, streets like the one they live in. Comfortable roads and avenues with lawns being mowed, cars washed, gardens tended, bikes ridden on concrete footpaths. Birds of paradise flaunt their orange petals and blue stamens, challenging the complacency of ordered flowerbeds. Speed humps and roundabouts with one-way signs, double yellow lines, roadworks — things are changing. Katherine smiles to herself. *William*.

They reach the strip of traditional shops: the greengrocer's with an array of apples, oranges, rockmelons; the butcher's display of lamb, beef, sausages; the florist overflowing with pink carnations, red roses, violets, golden daffodils. Cafe Smooth's austere modernism, its black and white colours and minimalist settings, contrast with the old-fashioned shops. Rachel drops her sister at the cafe.

The afternoon seems long and Katherine keeps looking at the white-faced clock. She serves an old lady Earl Grey tea. It gets busy then. After she gives the girl with a nose ring a banana smoothie, she notices it is already five o'clock. She starts cleaning up. At five-thirty, she locks the doors. Her pay is left in the till in an envelope. A shiver runs down her back as she opens the till and puts the notes in her purse. *Independence.*

The cook's clashing of pots and plates echoes through the tiled cafe floor. Katherine gets ready for her first date — the green top, make-up, perfume. *I'm nervous. I never thought anyone would ever ask me out. Does my hair cover my face? Do I look all right? I don't. Wish Rachel was here. She'd tell me if I look all right. Mum always says I'm beautiful, which is useless.* Katherine talks to the art deco mirror that hangs behind the cappuccino machine. *Why is William taking me out anyway? He's that good looking, he could ask anyone. I bet he won't turn up. No, that's stupid. He'll turn up because Greg's his friend. He doesn't like me. He didn't mean to ask me out. How could he be so cruel? I'm not going. When Jessie comes, I'll say I've got a cold. She'll just have to go without me.*

There's a knock on the cafe's closed door. Jessie's forehead is pressed against the glass. *You're early. It's only 5.45.* Katherine unlocks the door. Greg's standing behind Jessie and William's behind him. *Panic.*

'Are you ready, Katherine?'

'Yes.' Katherine calls out to the cook that she's going.

'Right,' echoes from the kitchen.

William stands awkwardly next to Greg. His hands are in his pockets. *Am I supposed to go up to him? What am I supposed to do?* Jessie threads her arm through Katherine's. 'What movie do you want to see?'

That is Greg's cue to say he wants to see *Batman* and Jessie's cue to argue that she'd like to see a 'meaningful' film. 'Batman's meaningful. He always gets the bad guys.'

'Sure.' Jessie's laughing. She unthreads her arm from Katherine's as she gets into Greg's car.

William and Katherine sit in the back seat. *Thank god for movies.* They talk about films. Katherine relaxes a little and William takes his hands out of his pockets. She glances at his eyes to check. *Hazel. I love hazel eyes.*

They end up seeing *Batman*. Katherine screams in the frightening parts and William takes her hand. Then he doesn't let it go. *Your hand is so big, sort of rough. Is that what men's hands are like?* She glances at him as the Batmobile races through Gotham City. *My stomach feels like butterflies. William. I really love your name and your hands.*

'You owe me coffee and cake after forcing me to see that, Greg,' Jessie complains as they walk down the red-carpeted stairs out of the cinema.

'Come on, you have to admit the special effects were fantastic. Virtual reality is ...'

'I know, fantastic.' Jessie puts her arm through Greg's. 'You're my crazy computer fanatic.'

The cinema complexes ooze people onto the street, everyone shoving as groups move one way or another. William takes Katherine's hand again. 'Don't want you to get lost.' They follow Jessie and Greg until the crowds ease and they can wander slowly past the shops which are still open at eleven — bookshops, music shops, cafes, game arcades with machines blaring colours and action. The scent of coffee draws them to a window layered with glass shelves. White meringues are piled high into a pyramid. Smooth dark chocolate covers the Sacher torte. Cherries and rich cream seep from the chocolate Bavarian. Thick lemon frosting layers the orange and poppyseed cake.

'Lemon meringue pie for me,' Jessie announces.

'Greedy.'

They sit at a table inside. 'I'll share if you're all nice to me.'

They eat lemon meringue pie and chocolate cake and drink frothy cappuccino while dissecting the technology involved in creating *Batman* and virtual reality. Greg and Jessie get caught up in talking about the latest computers.

'Do you want some more chocolate cake?' William asks.

Katherine shakes her head. 'Are you studying a lot now?'

'I'm supposed to be, but I keep thinking about after the exams, when I'm going north. I spend too much time at the beach.'

'I like the beach. I'm thinking of doing something in the surf. Maybe lifesaving.' But Katherine doesn't want to talk about herself or the little she knows about lifesaving. She pushes William's conversation into surfing stories of boards in big swells, riding too close to rocks and cliff faces, searching for the special wave, the lefthand tubes on a reef break. His hazel eyes glint with green and brown flashes as he talks about it. But it isn't bragging. It's something else, something to do with chasing the surf, catching that wave. Katherine hardly understands his freedom, but she senses the liberation of streets without footpaths, the bush, wild gardens of native flowers. *I want yellow wattle. Kookaburras. Golden butterflies.*

'The guys and I just stack our gear into a car, usually mine, and we go.'

*You're lucky. No mother telling you what to do. No hospitals. Just your mates. I bet you drink beer. I want to drink beer.* Katherine looks at her watch. Eleven-thirty. 'I have to be home by midnight.' She reaches into her bag to pay. 'I've got money now that I work,' she announces.

'Well, keep it. We're paying.' William stands.

'That doesn't seem fair.'

'Next time, you girls can pay. That's right, isn't it, Greg?'

'Next time.'

Greg and Jessie wait in the car as William walks Katherine to the door. She doesn't put the key into the lock because she knows her mother will be in the lounge room waiting for her, listening for the key. 'I had a good time, William.'

'Me too.' He brushes her hair away from her face, making her instinctively shudder. He bends his head towards her. She pulls her hair back over her face, wanting to hide when his lips touch hers. *Sweet. You taste so sweet. Chocolate and coffee.* She doesn't resist. He presses harder and she opens her mouth a little. His tongue presses into her mouth and it feels warm and tender. Then she closes her lips.

She puts the key in the lock. Turns around to watch him walk to the car, then turns away and goes inside. Her mother is watching television. An old Judy Garland movie. She's been crying and her eyes are red. 'Did you have a nice time?'

'Yes, Mum. We saw *Batman*.' Her mother starts to ask questions but Katherine interrupts. 'I'm tired. I want to go to bed. Goodnight, Mum.'

'Of course, *bambina*. We will talk in the morning. You go to your bed.'

'Goodnight, Mum.' Katherine shuts her bedroom door.

She changes into her nightie, gets comfortable under the covers, holds Pup. 'I'm seventeen and I've been kissed. I'm not the Beast tonight. Not tonight.'

# CHAPTER TEN

Katherine packs clothes, schoolbooks, the bits and pieces she needs for hospital. 'Pup, don't sit there just because you're stuffed.' She flings him into her bag. 'Sorry, I'm in a hurry.' She rings Jessie quickly, to remind her to take notes for the classes she'll miss.

Katherine crashes into the kitchen chairs, bumping Rachel who's eating toast and jam.

'Hey, calm down will you. I'll see you in hospital in a few days.' Rachel doesn't finish her breakfast. 'I'll bring you something nice to eat. We can be gluttons together. You'll be fine, you know.'

'Sure. Got to go.' Their mother is waiting in the car. She's not working today. Swapped her shift to be with Katherine, as always.

'Thanks, Mum.' Katherine throws her bag into the back seat.

In the morning light, her mother looks pale. She switches on the radio as they drive towards the hospital. 'Your Grandpapa and Nonna send their love to you.' Changing gears, she changes the subject. 'You lose too much time from school. If you miss too much school next year, it will be hard for you to get into Medicine.'

'I won't miss school next year. But this year I just *have* to have this operation and the other operations. You agreed, Mum. And ... there's the surgery on my face.'

'I wish ...' Her mother hesitates. 'You remember grafts can die ... and the Professor does not know if he can help you. There will be months in and out of the hospital and there is the recovery ...' She takes in a quick breath. 'You will be sick, Katherine.'

*I don't want to talk about it now.* 'Yes, Mum.' *I don't care about being sick, I've been sick before, and the hospital ... it's part of my life. I can't imagine what it'd be like not going there. I want to look normal. Mum, I know you're worried, but I've decided. It's what I want.*

Her mother chats lightly between songs playing on the radio. 'Rachel is helping her friend Jill with make-up at a wedding. She enjoys doing it after the dental work.' 'Old Mr Jones is still making his peas fly around the lunch room.' 'It was the right thing to give up the swimming. Study comes first and your arm had to be fixed. You will be able to move much better after this operation.'

Katherine answers occasionally, lapsing into her own thoughts. *I know you'll be there for me, for this and for the new operations, because I'm going to do it. Sometimes I hate the hospital. The surgery, being sick, the pain, the scarring, and when the grafts don't work. But the hospital means everything too, otherwise I wouldn't have long hair, I wouldn't be able to move my arm or have proper breasts. It's just that I want more ... to be ...* She stares out of the window, searching for butterflies between the eucalyptus trees. It's been raining lightly. Early autumn rain. The leaves of the eucalypts are glossy wet and beautiful. *I want to be Beauty. Not the Beast. Is that so greedy? After all that surgery ... can't I be Beauty?*

Katherine touches the side of her face. *The coach was so angry when I told him I wouldn't swim any more. He shouted that I'd wasted his time and I shouted back, 'You wasted mine.' Everyone heard. It was awful. I hate shouting, but do I feel bad about it?* She shakes her head. *No. He was wrong. I'm not a cheat. I just couldn't compete any more.*

'We're here, Katherine.' The hospital is large and familiar. Admissions. Forms to fill in. Details. Dates. Then corridors, nurse stations, lifts. The ward is always the same. Katherine feels strangely comfortable as her mother waits to tell the ward clerk that her daughter has arrived. Katherine slings her bag onto the white-sheeted bed with the stainless steel railings. *Home again.* She half laughs. *No kookaburras and gum trees, but home.*

Katherine unpacks her nighties and personal things. Pup rests on her pillow. He's here for her, for every operation. She kisses him. 'See, I still love you.' *William said he'd visit. I hope, hope, hope he does.*

Her mother looks at the phone next to the bed, then writes down the number. The sister recognizes Katherine. She jokes, 'I'm not sure if I'm glad to see you or not. Well, you know what to do by now.' There are her blood pressure and temperature to be taken, then more notes. Katherine's file is thick. Tattered pages mark well-used spots. 'Split thickness graft applied posterolateral section of left thigh, immobilization of graft, scars more hyperplastic . . .'

'Onto the scales, Katherine.' The sister writes figures on the form attached to the plastic clipboard.

Katherine grimaces. *I hate this. Fat, fat. Mum, don't you dare look.* The sister writes down Katherine's weight, talking about the weather. 'The rain's been a relief, hasn't it? You'd better change into this surgical gown. Not very glamorous is it? The anaesthetist will be in soon to talk to you. If you want me, just press the buzzer.' She touches Katherine's hand. 'Everything will be all right.'

The process begins. Separation from life outside. Trolleys carrying medicines and reports rattle along corridors. Beepers shrill as doctors race towards emergencies. Tearoom gossip wafts between shifts.

Flowers, visitors, food trays, gauze and bandages, patients ... the hospital hive.

Her mother flicks through a magazine while Katherine looks out of the window at businessmen frantically rushing across the road, mothers pushing strollers, lovers walking hand in hand towards the park, derelicts slouching against the old walls of the hospital.

It's another life inside the hospital walls.

*Books and coloured paper lie across the benches. Children are seriously colouring in with thick crayons. A young teacher is explaining a maths problem to a fourteen-year-old boy. Half hidden in a beanbag, a little girl with pigtails laughs at the story she's reading. Four kids are writing a play. An older girl stares out of the window.*

*A man comes into the room. He bends over the little girl in the beanbag and lifts her into her wheelchair. 'Time for your physiotherapy.' The little girl stops laughing.*

*In the morning the children's ward is always busy. Children who aren't critically ill, but who aren't allowed out of bed, play board games with children who are allowed out of bed. Some have assignments set by the hospital teacher. Kids with tubes in their noses, kids with drips attached to mobile units, kids with cancer and diabetes and cystic fibrosis and spina bifida play because they feel better today. Eight-year-old Katherine with no hair is drawing a picture of her mother and Rachel. Posters of the children's work are hung throughout the ward.*

*The nurses' station in the middle of the ward has a view of everything. Parents, nurses, doctors, social workers and teachers focus on the children, who are the centre of a private world within the ward. Visitors come in from time to time bringing presents and there are parties with balloons for birthdays. Mothers come in all the time and the children get individual attention which their brothers and sisters don't receive.*

*Sometimes disturbing things happen there. Parents challenge the system. They argue with the doctors and nurses, guarding their children against decisions they question. The children are afraid then.*

*Sometimes terrible things happen there. Children get very sick. Some never go home.*

*Katherine cries after her surgery. The skin of her back has been cropped for her graft. It's red and throbs and she vomits from the anaesthetic drugs. She calls for Mama, who holds her and stays throughout the night, and the nurses are kind and all the people in the ward are kind. Even though it hurts, she knows she's special and safe because they all look after her.*

*The ward is her home.*

The anaesthetist arrives. Katherine refuses the preoperative drugs that would calm her before she's wheeled into the operating theatre. The doctor discusses the procedures and fills in more forms before he leaves. 'I'll see you soon,' he says.

Katherine lies on the mobile bed. Cotton weave blankets are tucked around her like a cocoon. Pup's under her left arm. The orderly jokes as he pushes the bed around corners and passageways, the ceiling whizzing past as if she is on a rollercoaster ride. 'This is a Batman ride. I'm the Joker. Do you want to be Catwoman?'

'Catwoman? Maybe. I liked the Batman movie.' *And William.*

Katherine's mother walks fast alongside her daughter, like a guard against intruders, protecting Katherine from the onslaught of draughts and impersonal staff. They arrive. Heavy plastic sheets divide the operating theatres from the rest of the hospital. Her mother has special permission to go with Katherine into the inner sanctum.

The Professor is waiting. He's hard to recognise in his green surgical cap and gown; but Katherine knows it is him by the thinning tufts of hair protruding from his cap and by his eyebrows, which are white and bushy.

'Katherine, how are you?' His voice is concerned as he goes over the details once again. 'Are you still happy to have the skin cropped from the back of your thigh? You know we haven't taken skin from that section for a while.'

'I know, Professor.'

'Don't forget your arm will be in a splint when you wake up.'

She half smiles. 'I won't forget, Professor. I've had

a lot of practice at this.' *So much practice, but I'm getting closer. Just a few more operations.* 'What about my neck, my face?'

'We'll talk about that after this operation.'

Katherine looks disappointed.

'I'm going to try, Katherine, if you really want it. If your mother agrees.'

'I really want it.' The anaesthetist inserts a needle into the vein at the top of her hand. 'That needle hurts.' She hates the stinging liquid that burns into her hand, flooding into her arm like molten lava. Her stomach knots and the fears and memories she has before every operation erupt. She reaches out for her mother's soft jacket.

Her mother presses her fingers to her lips. 'I love you.'

Katherine starts to cry, but the tears lie quietly on her cheeks as she falls into unconsciousness.

Nothing. No time.

Fleetingly, Katherine opens her eyes. *Is it over?* She reaches for Pup. She sees her mother sitting in a grey vinyl chair next to the bed. *You're so young, Mama. Am I two? Six? Eight? Twelve? Fifteen? Are you young? Am I a baby? You're wearing the jacket.* Waves of nausea engulf Katherine. A nurse gently rolls her onto her left side, injecting an anti-vomiting drug into her thigh. The drip pumps fluid, salt, glucose into her vein. *Where's my arm? Have I got an arm? My leg. Where's my leg?*

\* \* \*

*Her mother is watching, helping, calming her baby as she has done every day for the past two months. Two-hourly, Katherine is turned by the nurse. Her small hands and arms and leg are mobilised gently. Katherine's dummy falls out but before she can cry the nurse pops it back into her mouth. Katherine's round face, with the feeding tube taped into her nose, momentarily brightens with a smile.*

*'You're beautiful, sweetheart, and I'm going to make sure you can move properly and that you get better. I know you don't understand.' The nurse strokes her cheek.*

*There is no pillow. Katherine lies stretched, her neck extended. The nurse rolls her over so she's lying straight. 'You want to hold your head up high one day, don't you?' The nurse turns to Katherine's mother. 'She has to go for another treatment today to remove the dead tissue. You understand, don't you?'*

*Katherine's mother is thin and pale. She whispers, 'Yes, but is she getting better?'*

*'Yes, much better,' the nurse answers softly as she pumps painkillers into the drip.*

Painkillers, nurses, her mother, doctors, all move in and out of Katherine's consciousness.

Then she's in the ward. Thick, white dressings around her arm so she can't move it. Thick, white dressings around her thigh where the skin has been cropped. Vomiting. Her mother brings water. Katherine passes water.

There are noises in the night. Torches flash through the ward and people call out, buzzers, the sister's face peering at Katherine. 'Are you all right?' Katherine doesn't answer, shifting restlessly, moaning quietly.

In the morning, tea and toast. Katherine feels better. The drip is taken out. The outer dressing is changed.

The Professor checks the thigh for infection. 'It looks good.' He examines under Katherine's arm, looking at the dressing over the graft. 'It all looks good, Katherine.' *I don't feel good. It hurts. Everything hurts so much. I hate hospital.*

Three days later, Katherine's playing poker with an off-duty orderly.

'You're too lucky at this for me.' He throws down his cards.

'Luck has nothing to do with it. I'm a great poker player.'

He laughs. 'All right. I've got to get to work now.'

The graft under her arm is thick and swollen. Her arm is splinted, bandaged and immobile so that movement doesn't tear it. The back of her thigh is crusted over like a huge scab. Sore, but getting better, and Katherine's happy. *Jessie's coming and Rachel and William. Where is my brush? Mirror? Great, I look like a ghost. I'll pinch my cheeks. That's better. Nightie. Ouch, my leg. Where's the blue nightie? Mum's always moving things. I can't stand it. Oh, there it is, in the cupboard. I like my nighties to be in the drawers, not in the cupboard. I'm glad Mum's back at work. She drives me crazy.* Katherine brushes her hair with her left hand, tugging at knots. She puts down her brush and runs her fingers along her shoulder, up her neck, through her hair. *I can't believe it, but Mum's said yes. I hoped she would. She's the best mother. And the Professor's said yes. He said he can't promise it will work, but it will work. I'm going to wear my hair up one day. I just know it. I am. I am.*

'Hi.' Rachel is standing there with an enormous chocolate Easter rabbit. Jessie's next to her with a pile of school work. William's behind them, looking embarrassed, holding yellow, pink and blue snapdragons.

## CHAPTER ELEVEN

Cleansing with soap and water. The warm liquid seems to seep inside the tightness of skin and muscle, washing away the stiffness and pain of the night. Katherine half listens to the nursing sister talk as the watery heat soothes and pampers. The young nurse tells her that she won her semi-finals in the local squash game and afterwards she went to a cheap Chinese restaurant with some of the team and her boyfriend. 'We had a noodle-sucking competition. The soy sauce was all over everyone's faces, especially my boyfriend's. He was the worst.' Katherine blinks, listening properly now. 'He's hopeless. Can you believe he didn't even pay for my chow mein?' *William paid for my cake and coffee after the movies, except I don't know if he's my boyfriend. He didn't say anything when he visited with Rachel and Jessie. I suppose Jessie talked so much he didn't have a chance. He laughed when Rachel ate both of the chocolate rabbit's ears. He doesn't know about my body, my face, my ...* Katherine raises her arm, rubbing under her hair.

The nurse grabs her arm. 'Don't move. You'll pull the graft.'

'Sorry. I wasn't thinking.'

The nurse plies lubricating ointment over the graft. 'I'll cover it after the Professor sees how it's healing. Onto your side. Is your thigh sore?'

Katherine nods as she manoeuvres herself around, turning her back on the nurse.

The nurse looks at the gauze mesh that was laid over the graft during surgery. The mesh is separating at the edges, which is a sign of healing. 'There's no swelling. All the gauze will be off in another few days.'

Katherine winces a little but she trusts the nurse, who clips the mesh with her sharp surgical scissors.

'I've finished with the dressing, Katherine. Oh, I saw something for you at the ward station.' She pushes the trolley loaded with its basins and gauzes towards the station, returning a few minutes later with a package. 'Hope it's something nice.'

'It's probably homework.' Opening it, Katherine laughs. She's received a few of these packages lately — Physics and Maths. 'I'm right. Homework.'

The nurse grins as she goes to her next patient.

Dear Katherine

'Come, come with me and we will make short work ...'

I think the Friar's wrong, don't you? *Romeo and Juliet* wasn't short work and this won't be either. But you must admit it was worth making the effort to understand Shakespeare.

I've put your next assignment inside this envelope — *to be byron. an anthology.* There are some interesting new poets represented in this collection. Have a look at V.V. Sipos's poem, *to be byron.* Her work is challenging, but you enjoy a challenge, don't you? We're all looking forward to you coming back to class and giving us your opinions. You always have a lot of them.

Get well soon.

Regards,

Mr Roberts

Katherine flicks through the collection. *I can't believe it. There are pages and pages of poetry. Mr Roberts, give me a break.*

The day is busy with physiotherapy, exercises, helping the nurses, phone calls.

Nonna rings. Katherine says a few Italian words to her Nonna to make her happy, but Nonna understands English. She's been studying English at a language school in Genoa.

'So I can speak to my grandchildren properly,' she says. 'I am trying to teach your grandfather also.'

'Are you *bene* ... better, Katherine? Speak louder, *cara*. Grandpapa is sending money to buy for you a pretty dress. You are not swimming, your mama tells to me. That is a great pity, but you will do this surf-lifesaving. This will be very good.'

*I can't wait until you visit at Christmas. Then we'll be like a real family. Money for a dress. Rachel will be so jealous. Jessie will have to come with me to choose.*

Jessie's phone call. 'You're so lucky you don't have a father. Dad went insane about Greg. Mum just hid in the kitchen as usual. She can't stand Dad shouting. Why can't I be like my good little sister she's asking, no, *telling* me. Well, I'm not my good little sister. Dad caught us in the car. We were only kissing. Who'd expect him to be snooping around at eleven at night? God, I hate him. Anyway, if he thinks I'm not going to see Greg, he's wrong. When are you coming home? I need a refuge. Well, at least on Saturday night.'

*Jessie, I don't know what a father is. The Professor's a father and he is wonderful. Mr Roberts isn't a father, but he'll be great when he is. I know that. There's Grandpapa, who's far away. My father ... Rachel says before he left, he used to buy us ice-creams. We'd eat them in the car, waiting for him to leave the pub. Is that a father? A dad? Sometimes I think I'd like to meet him. Ask him why he left Mum. Why he left us. Was it because of me?*

Rachel's phone call. 'It's a serious improvement not having towels and junk all over the bathroom floor, Katherine. The information on surf-lifesaving arrived. You have to do your Bronze Medallion to be allowed to get onto a patrol team. It looks hard. You've got to be really fit. I'll bring in the information today. By the way, some of your friends from the swimming team rang. I told them you're not training any more, but they want to talk to you. So you have to phone them. Jessie left some study notes for you that I'll bring in. That's it. So I'll see you tonight then.' *I'd be scared if you weren't around, Rachel.*

Her mother's phone call. 'No, I have not forgotten. I will bring some paper and pens. What treatment have you had? The graft, is it healing? What about your leg? What did the doctor say about coming home . . .?'

*Question, questions, questions. I love you, Mum, but you give me a headache sometimes.*

William's phone call. 'I'm supposed to be studying but I haven't done much of it. At least you've got an excuse not to. The surf's been fantastic on the peninsula. When you're out of there, maybe you'd like to come for a drive up the coast to have a look.'

*He rang. He talked to me. He knows I'm in the hospital and he doesn't care. Maybe he likes me. He's so cute looking. Will Mum let me go? Sure she will. Anyway, it's my choice. He definitely likes me. At least, I think he does.*

Medication, meals, medical students' visits, dressings, blood taken, playing cards, night rounds and sometimes time to hide in a quiet corner. Katherine opens in the middle of *to be byron*.

*theatrically he reads,*
*byronic, passionate,*
*a little sweat dripping*
*dropping insecurities*
*wiped clean on a handkerchief.*

Katherine shudders. *I can feel that. A Byron, but not a great Byron. Exposing your feelings to a crowd. Are we supposed to laugh at you? I don't want to laugh at you. I've sweated too. I think you're brave.* She closes the book. *Another time, Mr Roberts.*

It is afternoon when her mother hurries in. She kisses Katherine and gives her the writing paper and pens she wants. 'You look much better, *bambina*.'

'I am, Mum.'

Her mother consults the ward sister over the treatments Katherine has had today, discussing her daughter's physiotherapy program and progress. She checks the time that the Professor will be in for his rounds before fussing around the drawers and bed tray. When she starts rearranging William's snapdragons, Katherine forces her eyes shut. *Stop it, Mum. Stop it. Leave my things alone. I can't stand it.*

Katherine opens her eyes with a start when Rachel drops the surf-lifesaving information, phone numbers of the swimming team and Jessie's study notes onto her bed. Rachel laughs and drops the photo album she's carrying onto the bed too. 'I have to tell you about last Saturday when I helped Jill on her wedding job. It was chaotic. There were five bridesmaids to do, as well as the bride.'

'You should have been a beautician.' Katherine runs her fingers through her hair. 'You're good at doing hair as well.'

'Only yours, Katherine. You'd never let anyone else touch your hair except me. Not even Mum.'

A shiver runs downs Katherine's back. 'That's true. I'd forgotten.'

'Anyway, let me tell you about the wedding. I even got paid for it.'

'What a show-off.' Katherine laughs affectionately.

'Can you believe that Jill's asked me to help her with another wedding? All I had to do was put some touch-up powder on the bridesmaids and thread sprays of white blossoms through their hair. My dress and hands and everything smelt of jasmine. It was like being in Mum's garden except better because I heard all the gossip about who's going out with whom and what the groom does and the dating and everything. They must have thought I was part of the family.'

Their mother leaves William's snapdragons and sits beside Rachel, next to Katherine's bed. Opening the album, they study the photographs. The bride is beautiful in her white gown of beaded satin and her flowing veil. The groom's eyes are glazed red by the flashing lights or maybe by the shock of marriage and commitment. There are fathers and mothers and relatives and guests from generations of family and friends. Nostalgia fills the air between them as they share a family occasion that will never be theirs. A father, husband ...

'Your grandparents will be here for Christmas,' their mother reminds them and they feel comforted.

'We have a family too, Mum.' Katherine nods her head.

'Yes.'

They are quiet for a while.

Rachel digs in her bag and pulls out a packet of chocolate and coconut marshmallows. 'I brought these. Your favourite.'

Katherine shakes her head. 'I'm dieting.'

'Just have one, Katherine.'

'I have lost a bit of weight from the effects of the anaesthetic.' Katherine takes a marshmallow. Rachel and their mother do too and so does the sister and the wardsman who wanders in and the tea lady who's announcing afternoon tea. It's a party. The wardsman tells rude jokes until Katherine's mother tells him off, laughing so much that everyone knows she doesn't mean it.

Everything stops for the afternoon rounds. Ward staff wait in anticipation. Patients look anxiously towards the door. The Professor is followed into the ward by a squad of students who peck after him like chicks, all jumpy and young, fighting for their rightful places. There is an understanding between the Professor and Katherine. She's an interesting case study for the students. The Professor has already briefed them on her history and she's agreed to be 'interesting'. She answers the students' questions, lets them look at her scars and new graft, lifts up her hair when they want to see her hidden scars.

In return, the Professor sponsored her school work-experience program last term; she followed him on his rounds where he answered her questions, where she scrubbed up and watched him perform miraculous surgery. The Professor promised to help her try to get into medical school. He'll write a letter supporting her application and act as a referee when it's the right time. 'But there are no guarantees,' he says.

Secretly, Katherine believes the Professor is what all men should be like. Secretly, she wants to be just like him.

'The surgical team is preparing for your next operation, Katherine. We've scheduled it for a few months' time, after your mid-year exams. You'll miss most of the remainder of the year.'

'I'll make up for it.'

'Are you prepared?'

'Yes,' both Katherine and her mother answer together.

# CHAPTER TWELVE

Katherine burrows under her freshly washed blanket. Autumn breezes drift through her window as she peers from under the covers. She can just see kookaburras sitting on the bare clothesline. Growls bristle from the lounge room. Lions on a wildlife special, her mother's favourite. Katherine imagines her mother warming herself in front of the fire, slowly drinking milky espresso from her hand-crafted mug patterned with swirls of cream and sea-green. There's a chip in the mug. Katherine had been only little when she knocked it over. She'd been playing ball with Rachel in the lounge room. 'I'm sorry, Mama, Kath'rine sorry,' her child's voice pleaded. Katherine hides under her blanket, trying to shake away the memory.

Her mother had been inconsolable, crying and crying. 'Can't I have anything for myself? I am so tired. Tired. Can't I ... even have my coffee cup for myself?' Her words jumbled into sobs: 'father', 'alone', 'hospital', 'doctors', 'alone', and Katherine and Rachel hadn't understood, cowering in the corner because their mother was always strong and brave. *I understand now, Mum. It's better now, isn't it, Mum?*

Rachel's CD murmurs softly as she moves around her room putting out clothes for tomorrow. Katherine calls out to her sister. 'Remember, you promised to give me a lift to school.' *I've missed so much school even with the extra work from the teachers. There are going to be so many things to catch up on. And I just know the swimming squad are going to be angry with me.*

'I won't forget, Katherine. See you in the morning.' *Rachel never forgets anything, but I do. That Physics assignment Jessie gave me in hospital was awful. I couldn't remember how to do any of it. I'm useless.* Katherine grabs Pup. *Stop thinking. Go to sleep. I'm scared, that's all. I'm always scared going back to school after hospital. It'll be okay. I'll be okay.* Carefully reaching for the bed-light, Katherine stretches her right arm. *That feels better. I can move. It's safe in hospital. I'm safe at home, but tomorrow's different.*

As usual, Jessie is waiting for Katherine at the school gate. 'Great to see you back. You've got to let me sleep over on Saturday night. I've told Greg I'm staying with you already and I've got things organised.' Jessie burbles on about her father and Greg and the Physics assignment and Greg and school and Greg and ... Greg.

Katherine interrupts. 'Aren't you glad to see me?'

'Of course I am.'

'I'm not so sure. It sounds like you're just glad you might have a place to stay on Saturday night.'

'That's mean. Really mean. You know Dad's been tough on me about Greg. I've been dying for you to come back to school. Anyway, I can stay at Liz's on Saturday night.'

'You don't even know what tough is. I just came out of hospital, remember?'

'You're so sarcastic, Katherine,' Jessie huffs. 'Sorry if I've said the wrong thing.'

'I'm not sarcastic. It's just that you're pretty self-centred, don't you think?'

'No, I don't think.' Jessie picks up her bag and heads toward the classroom, refusing to look at Katherine. Her blonde ponytail flicks from side to side as she stomps across the bitumen.

Katherine walks behind her. 'Come on, Jessie.'

'Well, I was happy to see you and it wasn't just because of Greg.'

'It would've been nice to ask me how I am and maybe tell me what's been happening at school first. Slow down will you, Jessie?'

'No, I won't. I'm not self-centred. That's unfair. Who wrote notes for you at school? Who visited you in the hospital? And who got the notes to you? Who phoned you every day?'

Katherine hesitates. 'I guess, you did.'

'Greg's important to me now, that's all. My dad's giving me a rotten time. I was going to ask you how you are, you know that.'

'Will you slow down?'

Jessie stops suddenly. She's scowling. 'All right.'

'This is stupid, but I suppose I started it.'

'You did.'

'You know how I am when I come back to school after the hospital.'

Jessie shakes her head. They stand there glaring at each other until Katherine bites her lip. 'I was wrong. Sorry. Don't stay at Liz's. You know she drives you crazy with all her causes. She'll lecture you all night about being a vegetarian or saving the ants from extinction or something. You'll end up eating tofu and you hate tofu.'

Jessie puts her hands on her hips. 'I don't mind tofu with chilli sauce.'

'Come on. Stay at my place on Saturday night. I knew I was going to be hopeless today. Sorry.'

As Jessie heads for the lockers, she turns around to Katherine with a gratified look. 'It's nice when you've done the wrong thing, not me. All right, I'll stay at your place on Saturday.'

People call out 'hello', 'glad to see you back', 'you look great', as Katherine enters the classroom. The restless scraping of chairs against the grey linoleum floor indicates that Mr Roberts is late as usual. He dashes into the classroom, tosses his book onto the front desk, looks around the room quickly. 'I see you've returned, Katherine. I hope you're well and fit and ready to resume our study of literature?'

'Yes, Mr Roberts. Thanks very much for all the work you sent me in hospital.' She rolls her eyes.

Everyone laughs.

'She speaks. O, speak again, bright Katherine, for thou art glorious to this class.' Mr Roberts picks up his poetry book. 'Nice to have you back. I promise I won't make you "speak" today. I'll give you time to catch up. The rest of you have no excuses. Now to the poetry of our bright, new poets. We'll begin with "to be byron".'

Books open, papers shuffle, pens are raised. Katherine has to share her book with Jessie. 'Too busy planning Saturday to have your poetry, Jessie?' she whispers.

'Very funny. Shush, he's starting.'

*'he's read before*
*alone at night,*
*his work unpublished*
*fingered in his desk drawer*
*but will they laugh*
*... (at me)?*

*'black collarless shirt,*
*tight blue jeans,*

*pub lights squinting*
*crinkled eyes*
*but will they laugh*
*... (at me)?*

*'he peers into the crowd*
*then down*
*at floorboards scratched*
*and splintered*
*i'm afraid.'*

Katherine listens for a while to Mr Roberts questioning students about rhyme and rhythm, repetition, imagery, rhetorical questions: 'but will they laugh?' 'i'm afraid.' The words circle inside her thoughts. She re-reads the section, trying to stop the thoughts shifting inside her head. *It's all right to be afraid. I know what it's like to be afraid.* Katherine pushes her finger against the words on the page. *And guess what? Some people laugh. I've been laughed at. You've just got to keep trying.* Suddenly, she's perspiring. Beads of sweat collect under her eyes. She touches the wetness, then presses her hand against her right side. She senses the dryness of her skin even though she smoothed cream over her skin as she does every morning, every day, every week, month, year. *What have you been through, anyway? Nothing. How'd you like being called girl who has to hide? Hide in a paper bag? Where's your courage?* Katherine stands up. Jessie whispers. 'Are you all right?'

'I hate this poem. Need some air.'

'I'll go with you.' Jessie starts to get up.

'No. Please, don't. I want to be by myself. If Mr Roberts asks, tell him I just need some air. Please, be a friend. Please.'

Jessie nods uncertainly. 'Okay, if that's what you want.'

Katherine leaves the room, moving past the desks, excusing herself to Mr Roberts quietly. She sees him approach Jessie, asking if everything's all right. Outside the classroom door she takes deep breaths before walking along the corridor, climbing up the stairs, climbing ... climbing until she reaches the out-of-bounds rooftop. Tobacco smells connect Katherine to the smokers and liars who always hide there. No one is on the rooftop now. She leans over the metal railing. The cold steel makes her skin goosebump, but her arms don't goosebump. She rubs her hand over her arms, rubbing, rubbing but she can only feel the dullness of scars. She surveys the school, its old brick classrooms and new Science block made of concrete and aluminium. A stretch of grass separates the buildings. Katherine stares at the grass scattered with clover patches and occasional white daisies.

Girls and teachers walk easily along the pebbled pathway across the grassy lawn to and from the old classrooms and the new Science block. *It's easy for all of you, isn't it? You just walk on the path. There are no great big potholes, are there?* Katherine watches the tops of girls' heads, some with ribbons knotted around plaits, some with short hair that clings onto their scalps, some with blonde and brown and red and black hair. She flicks her hair back like Jessie would. *I'm so tired of potholes.* She hears a laugh as a girl runs into a classroom. Clenching the metal railing, Katherine suddenly calls out, 'Unfair.' A few heads look up searching for the voice, but Katherine jumps back, away from the railing so they can't see her. *Stop it, stop it, Katherine. I'm just nervous. It's the surgery, leaving hospital, facing all the missed work. The stupid poem. That poet may be afraid to get what he wants, but I'm not. There is a path and it may be really hard to walk along, but I've decided. I'm not a coward. I've got things to do with my life.* She turns away from the railing, slides her feet against the concrete slab, pushes open the heavy fire door with its lighted EXIT sign. There are other classes.

'Are you feeling all right now?' Jessie's relieved when Katherine joins the other girls on their lunchtime hill. Jessie offers her apricots.

'Yes.' Everyone asks Katherine how she is after the operations, until she's annoyed. 'I'm fine. Can we talk about something more interesting? Exams for example.'

There is laughing. '*Very* interesting.'

'So when are you coming back to swimming training? We lost the last relay,' a team-mate accuses.

'Come on, Katherine's been in hospital and she doesn't have to swim if she doesn't want to.' Jessie defends her.

'Have you heard of free choice?' As usual, Liz leads the battle with heated arguments over who cares about swimming and school teams and rules.

'Thank god for Liz,' Jessie whispers, nudging Katherine. 'That so-called swimming mate is pretty ignorant.'

'No, I'm the ignorant one. Sorry about this morning.' Katherine half smiles. 'I'm just going through my "adjustment" period, as the Professor would say. That means I'm a bit confused. I'm better now.'

'What a relief. So can I tell you what I've organised for us?'

Katherine nods.

'There's a concert on Saturday night that you have to come to.'

'You're joking. I don't think it'll be very romantic, do you? The three of us. Greg, you and me.'

'William will be there, too.'

'How do you know?'

'Don't ask the details, just thank me. He's going to ring you.'

'Jessie, you're too much.'

'You mean, too terrific.'

Katherine takes an apricot. 'That's right. You're terrific.'

## CHAPTER THIRTEEN

Katherine's mother puts down the receiver. Fiddling with her hair, she twirls it into wispy curls. She stares out into her garden. Suddenly she turns away from the trees and their falling leaves. 'Katherine, Rachel,' she calls quietly. Then louder, 'Katherine, Rachel.'

Rachel emerges from her room with silver foils in her hair, but there is no sign of Katherine. The sound of hard rock comes from her room. Her mother knocks, then opens the door. Katherine's lying on her bed, studying English. Shouting above the music, her mother calls out, 'I want to talk to you about something.'

Startled, Katherine jumps up, then objects, but her mother's voice is urgent. 'Please, Katherine.'

'All right, all right. I need a break anyway.'

Rachel makes coffee and opens a packet of chocolate mint biscuits. She hands her mother her sea-green cup, puts the biscuits on the small table next to the lounge, then settles into a chair, sipping her own coffee. Katherine grabs a mint biscuit before she slumps onto the lounge. They watch their mother pacing the carpeted floor between pot plants and chairs. She stops for a moment, stripping dry leaves and petals from the vase of roses on the mantelpiece. Leaning against the mantelpiece, her hands full of dying leaves, she faces the girls. 'Your father rang. He wants to see you both.'

They stare at her for a while. Katherine edges back into the lounge trying to get comfortable. Then Rachel speaks, struggling with memories of him. 'Why?'

Her mother shakes her head. 'I do not know. It has been so long.'

Katherine's quiet. *My father? What does that mean? My father? After all this time.* She bites her lip. *I don't remember him.* Playing with the edge of the old lounge, she pulls out threads. *I don't know who my father is.* She wraps a long thread around her finger. 'What was he like, Mum?'

Her mother hesitates, then smiles at Rachel. 'I have told you before. Young, beautiful, like Rachel.' She coughs. 'But too young to be married with children. Like me, too young. He liked the bush.' Her mother closes her eyes.

*I like the bush too.*

They wait for her to continue.

'A geologist. That is a beautiful thing to be, working with the rocks, walking in khaki shorts and a shirt in the hot sun in the red deserts. He loved the outback of this country.' She wipes her eyes. 'Me, also. He took me many times into the country and we camped beside little creeks with rocks and he made a fire to boil for his billy tea.'

She whispers. 'I loved him.'

'I don't remember that, Mum,' Rachel says.

'No, he changed after the babies. Terrible changes. He did not like the city and he had to wear a suit and go into an office.' She hesitates. 'We argued because he was late home, and he smelt of alcohol. Not the sweet smell of village wine after dinner shared with a family. Different.'

Rachel leaves her coffee cup and biscuits to stand beside her mother. She puts her hands over her mother's hands.

'Your grandfather was right. He was different to me. I should not have run away with him. A stranger. Afterwards there were the burns, hospitals, everything ... he left. I do not know why he wants to see you now. You must decide what you want.' She presses the dried rose petals into the palms of her hands. 'I cannot see him.'

*The cufflinks on his suit reflect the hallway light bulb. His feet stumble along the floorboards, making shadows that darken the corner. The mother tucks the baby safely into her cot. 'Shush, sleep darling. Shush.' Four-year-old Rachel clings to her mother's skirt. 'Rachel, let go of my skirt. You go to bed.' Nervously looking towards the hallway, her mother's voice whispers sharply. 'Rachel, you do as you are told. Let go.' The little girl cries, but her mother's hands are hard, forcing her into the bed with its Cinderella quilt and fairytale night-light. Rachel is afraid of the dark. Shutting the door quickly, the mother waits outside the girls' room.*

*'What are you staring at?' the man asks roughly.*

*'Where have you been?'*

*'None of your bloody business.' Alcohol reeks from his breath. 'Get me some food.'*

*'Get it yourself.'*

*'Bloody bitch.' He stands with his feet apart. His heavyset build dominates the room as he saunters towards her and the girls' bedroom door. 'I'm saying 'night to them.'*

*'You are not. You are drunk. They are afraid.' She manages to turn the bedroom key before he pushes her aside, forcing her against the door so that the doorknob presses into her spine.*

Their mother closes her eyes as she speaks. 'You must choose if you wish to see him. For me, he is the past and I must leave him there. He will telephone again.' She goes into her garden.

Katherine loses her job at Cafe Smooth when she admits that she's having more surgery later in the year. 'We're sorry, but it's just too much time away. We'll give you casual work when it comes up.'

Saturdays are now free; 'And I'm broke,' Katherine complains to Jessie. *And I'm dependent again.* Jessie's glad because she can come over earlier 'to study', or so she tells her father.

Jessie's father usually works on Saturdays, but not this Saturday. He has a new car and he drives Jessie over to Katherine's place. As he talks to Katherine's mother on the front verandah, he waves his arms enthusiastically, expanding his view of education, one of his regular topics. 'It's important for the girls to do well in these exams. Education is the way to the top.' He's slightly-built like Jessie, but he seems bigger than life with animated arguments that impress Katherine's mother. When he notices Jessie shaking her head, he laughs. 'Fine, I'm usually the one in a hurry, but I see you are today. I'll leave you girls with this one thought. When your teacher asks you, "How were your exam questions?" I hope you've got a better response than, "The exam questions were easy, it was only the answers that were a problem."'

Laughing, he dashes towards his car, calling out, 'Study,' before he drives away.

'Sure, Dad,' Jessie mutters.

'Your father is right, Jessie.' Katherine's mother picks up her garden fork and spade, heading for her roses.

'I can't help it, but I think your dad's sort of nice.' Katherine watches Jessie's father zoom down the street in his sleek sports car.

'That's the trouble. Everyone thinks Dad's great, but it's not like that. He puts so much pressure on me to get good, no, fantastic grades. You know, he thinks I won't study if I have a boyfriend. If he knew I was going out with Greg tonight, I'd really get it. Dad is so controlling, but I just can't keep lying to him.'

*Controlling? Mum's like that. Will I lie to her one day, like you lie? I don't want to. I'm glad I have my mother. Why aren't you glad to have a father? At least you have one.*

Jessie follows Katherine inside. 'We've got to do some study. It's my deal with Mum. I can go out with William as long as I do my work first and,' Katherine shakes her head, 'as long it's with a group. You and Greg are the group.'

'Luckily I like being a group.'

'Honestly, how old does Mum think I am?'

Katherine drags out her work. 'I hope you brought the Physics assignment.'

They organise themselves in Katherine's bedroom with the CD playing in the background, Katherine on the bed as usual and Jessie lounging on the floor. There are important discussions about the concert, Greg, exam nerves, surgery, William. 'Do you think he really likes me, Jessie?'

'Guys are difficult to work out. He wanted to come to the concert with you. He came to the hospital didn't he? So he likes you.'

'Yes, but he doesn't really know me.'

'Do you know him?'

'Guess I don't.'

They open their Physics books. Katherine slides off the bed to lie next to Jessie on the carpet. Notes, the assignment, books, are all carefully laid out in preparation. There is always a bit of initial nervousness when the deductive logic and analysis of Physics confronts them. Then they really start exploring the questions until they're engrossed in discovering scientific phenomena and answers.

When Rachel opens Katherine's door, they're surprised at how late it is. 'Do you want to hear about my second wedding job today or are you too busy studying? It was peculiar.'

'We've finished, haven't we, Katherine? My brain's tired. It's nearly time for dinner anyway. So what happened?'

Rachel sits on the bed. 'The wedding was in the park. You know, with a celebrant under a tree and birds twittering around.'

'We get the picture, Rachel.'

She smiles. 'I was trying to help Jill give the final touches to the bride's and bridesmaids' make-up before the ceremony except there were these gusts of wind. One caught the bride's dress. She looked as if she was going to take off like a great white balloon.'

'Is that the peculiar bit?'

'No, just wait, Katherine, I'll tell you. There was this dog, a brown-spotted mutt with yellow teeth. It started sniffing up the bride's dress which was still blown up like a balloon. She tried and tried to escape, but the dog wasn't going to stop. It kept sniffing until people started yelling, then chasing the stupid thing away. The mother of the bride was screaming at it to leave her daughter alone. The pageboy spat his chewing gum at it, but the dog just ate it, which was pretty funny. Anyway, in the end the groom got so angry that he took off his shoe and threw it at the dog. Guess what? The dog ran away with it! The groom had to get married without a shoe.'

'That's crazy, Rachel.'

'Yeah. I'm starting to think weddings are.'

At dinner the story of the dog gets wilder and wilder. The brown mutt now has ferocious teeth and he digs holes the size of craters to trap the bride. The groom ends up throwing his jacket and shirt and trousers at the dog and running around in his underpants.

'This is getting as good as my stories at work,' their mother laughs.

'You mean that those stories aren't true, Mum?'

'I am saying nothing.' She grins as she dishes out ravioli.

Dinner ends, dishes are washed, the kitchen is tidied. Jessie's changing into a dress her parents wouldn't approve of. Her mother takes Katherine aside. 'You look pretty tonight.'

'Thanks, Mum.'

'But be careful about moving your arm too much.'

'Mum, can you leave me alone?'

'You are not used to going out.'

'You mean with guys? Don't worry.'

'Katherine, you are only just out of the hospital. Does William understand that he has to be careful?'

'Am I a medical case?'

'No, of course not. It is not that. You do not understand men and what they want.'

'Are you talking about my arm or sex, Mum?'

'Please, Katherine.'

'It's because of my father coming back, isn't it?'

Just as she says that Jessie enters the room. Her short maroon dress clings to her like plastic wrap.

'You look terrific,' Katherine says but her mother shakes her head. The doorbell rings.

'I will get it.' Determinedly, her mother opens the front door. 'Come in.' It sounds like an order. Rachel escapes to the kitchen.

'Would you like a drink?' she asks Greg and William.

'No, we're right, thanks,' they echo each other.

'Come and sit down for a while. You are not in a rush are you?'

'Well, the concert starts at seven-thirty.' Greg looks at his watch.

'Good, there is some time. I'll bring you lemonade.'

Greg smiles. 'Lemonade?' He goes over to Jessie. 'You look great.'

Katherine's mother returns with the drinks giving one to Greg, then to William. 'You will be careful won't you? Katherine has not been out of hospital for long.'

William coughs as he drinks the lemonade. 'Sure.'

'She will have more surgery soon, for more grafts on her shoulder and face.'

*Mum, don't tell him about that. He doesn't even know what I hide under my hair. Why are you telling him?* Katherine glances at William, who's shifting uncomfortably in his chair.

'What do your parents do, William?'

'My dad's a plumber. He owns his business and Mum does the accounts.'

'So you want to be a teacher?' 'Where do you live?' 'Do you have a car? I hope you drive carefully.' 'What are your interests?' 'I hear you like basketball.' 'What subjects are you doing?'

Katherine looks towards the kitchen. Rachel is standing at the door, shaking her head. *I can't believe you're doing this, Mum. What's wrong with you? Who do you think William is? He's not my father. I'm not going to run away with him. Stop, Mum, stop.*

Katherine looks at Jessie, who shrugs helplessly. *I've got to do something.* 'Mum, can I have some more lemonade?' 'Mum, we've got to leave.' 'Mum, is something burning?'

Her mother ignores her, bombarding William with more questions. 'So you like surfing?' 'How do you have time to study and surf?' 'When will you bring Katherine home?'

*Mum, he's going to abduct me. Can't you see? Is William a blood-sucking vampire? Mum, please stop.*

But her mother doesn't stop asking. *I'll never forgive you for this. I've got to say something.* 'Mum, we're going now and we'll be back when the concert finishes.'

Her mother starts again but Katherine has already grabbed her jumper and her bag. 'Let's go.' She shoves Jessie in front of her. 'We're out of here. 'Bye Mum. Come on, let's go.' Her mother follows them to the door but they hurry and pile into William's old Valiant.

Jessie and Katherine stare at each other before bursting into a laughing fit. They can hardly speak. 'That was the worst.'

'Horrible.'

'Terrible.'

William changes gears. 'It wasn't that funny.'

'No, it was awful.' Katherine's nearly choking with laughter. 'I don't know why I'm laughing ... it was so awful ... but it was funny.'

Jessie nods. 'I've never seen that side of your mum.' They both stop laughing.

'Me neither.' *Me neither.* As the big old car turns onto the expressway, Katherine looks at William. 'I'm really sorry. Mum's not usually like that.'

'It was rough.' William concentrates on the road, the radio blares, Greg's arm is around Jessie as they talk quietly in the back until they don't talk any more.

Finding a car space is difficult, as William's nineteen-year-old Valiant needs one and a half spaces.

They end up driving around in circles until they find a spot in a dark alleyway marked No Standing. 'This'll do. Just right. I won't get a parking ticket. No one comes here.'

'No wonder.' Jessie looks around. 'Anyone could get mugged. This is an alleyway, you realise.'

'Don't worry, we're here. We'll protect you,' Greg reassures them, laughing.

Jessie hits his arm. 'You'll need protection in a minute.'

'Come on, we'll be late.'

'Do you go to hospital a lot?' William asks Katherine about the new operation and the operations she's had before. She answers briefly, trying to change the subject. *I don't want to talk about this. You're going out with me, not a hospital case. How could Mum tell you about my scars? You can see enough of them anyway. I was going to explain things after we got to know each other, not straightaway. I thought you were going to choke on that lemonade when she blurted it all out. How could she?*

'I guess your mother's protective about you.' Afterwards William doesn't say anything more as he walks beside Katherine to the concert hall.

*Say something. I can't. William, why don't you hold my hand? You did before. I want you to hold my hand.* She glances at him, but he's looking straight ahead.

Inside the round building thousands of people are jostling each other, searching for the right entry door.

Hawkers are selling hats and CD's for huge prices. 'We go in here.' Jessie hurries towards the entry, with Greg behind her. A lady takes their tickets and points to the gods. They start climbing. 'How far up are these seats?' Jessie asks suspiciously.

'Keep climbing. We'll get a great overview.'

'You're kidding.'

'Keep climbing. They were the only tickets left.'

'I don't think there's much further to go unless we're sitting on the roof.' Jessie pretends to pant. 'Oxygen! We're here. It is the roof.'

'Here's some oxygen.' Greg gives her a long kiss, making William smile and Katherine look away.

William and Katherine sit next to each other, separately. A low rumble starts moving through the crowds. 'They're coming.' Jessie leans forward. Lights start to flicker, the TV monitor blares, smoky grey puffs float across the audience. There are screams as the band surges onto the stage, grasping microphones, belting out electronic songs, crashing drums.

Music rocks the stage, filling the hall, reaching up to the gods. The crowds stand, swaying their hands, shouting. Jessie's pumping the air. Greg's pumping the air. William's pumping the air. Katherine pretends. *I'm not different, William. I'm like Jessie. See, I have long hair, but my eyes aren't blue like hers. They're brown. Do you like brown eyes? You kissed me. Remember?* Greg's arm is around Jessie. *But I'm not like Jessie am I? I am different. I don't want to be. I don't. I don't.*

# CHAPTER FOURTEEN

William drops them all off at Katherine's house. He doesn't walk Katherine to the front door. Haltingly, he rubs his hand over the lambswool seat covers. 'I'm surfing up the coast tomorrow. Meeting the guys at six. So I have to get going.'

Katherine sees her mother is waiting. 'Like a piranha,' Katherine whispers under her breath.

'The concert was great.' Jessie nudges Greg. 'I feel like a walk, otherwise I won't be able to get to sleep.'

'I need a walk too.'

'Do you want to come, Katherine?'

*What would you do if I said yes? Sometimes your games are irritating, Jessie. Just be honest. You and Greg want to be together, alone, outside, lying under a tree, watching the stars, kissing, touching each other. I understand because I want it too, but who'd want to touch me?* 'No thanks. I'm tired.'

It's after three when Jessie tiptoes into the bedroom. Katherine has left a night-light on for her. There is a mattress on the floor. Katherine holds her quilt close to her face so that Jessie doesn't know she's awake and watching her. Grass bits flake onto the carpet as Jessie unzips her maroon dress. It slides to the floor. She unclips her lacy white bra and drops it next to her dress. Her skin is smooth, perfect except for a reddish bruise on her right breast. As she leans towards the light, her breasts gently undulate, soft and round with erect pink nipples fully formed. Jessie switches off the light.

Katherine stares at the empty black space. Under her quilt, she feels her smooth breast with its circular nipple, imagining William exploring it with his hands, his mouth sucking ... Slowly Katherine creeps her hand onto her right side, ridged with scars and hardness. But it's William's hand pressing the ridged skin, searching for her girlish nipple. *I can't feel you touching me. It's dull, fuzzy. Oh yes, I feel you. William, you're pushing too hard. Too much. Hurting. Don't ... you're too rough.* Katherine edges away from her quilt, grappling with feathers and down. *It's not there. You can't find it. Don't ... stop, please ... There's no nipple, no ...* and William stops, horrified. Katherine closes her eyes. Crying quietly, she forces herself into restless sleep. Fathers and mothers, William and hairy beasts crisscross the night, searching for the morning.

\* \* \*

It's nearly midday when Katherine opens her eyes. Jessie's still sleeping. Katherine rolls onto her side, exhausted.

'Jessie. Katherine.' The voice repeats their names again and again, nagging sleep away. 'You must get up. It is lunchtime already.'

'Right, Mum.' Katherine sees her mother open the door. She leans out of her bed and pushes Jessie's arm. 'We're getting up.' *I really don't want to talk to you, Mum.* 'You don't have to wait for us.' She gets up and shuts the door.

Yawning, Jessie stretches her arms. 'Best night. I'm so lucky. Greg's training a lot for basketball, so he's really lean but strong.' She smiles. 'Very sexy.'

'You came back pretty late.'

'Yes, I did.' Jessie hugs her pillow.

'I'm not going to ask what you did last night.'

'And I'm not telling.' Laughing, Jessie gets up. She grabs the towel Katherine left out for her. 'Can I have a shower first?' Without waiting for an answer, she's out of the door and in the bathroom. Then there's the sound of water splashing and Jessie humming.

The afternoon consists of sandwiches and revision of *Romeo and Juliet* and talk about last night. 'I'm not really that interested in William.' Katherine pushes aside a pile of papers, looking for her poetry book.

'Why? I thought you liked him. What about his hazel eyes?' Jessie bites into a red apple.

The crunching grates on Katherine's nerves, but she ignores it and the lie. 'He likes his car too much.'

*William doesn't want to go out with me. It's the operations. My burns.* 'He hardly talked because he's too interested in surfing and fixing up his old Valiant.'

'Guys and their sports and cars. Greg's like that too. Sometimes I think he likes basketball better than me. I'm lucky that he hasn't got a car yet.' That starts Jessie on Greg and the topic of William subsides into mild interest, then nothing.

'Jessie, we'd better get on with the poetry.'

'One week, then exams. I think I'll do really well. Then I can tell Dad about Greg. I can't keep hiding him and don't want to anyway.' Jessie opens the anthology of poetry. 'Dad should be grateful for Greg. I've stopped partying since going out with him. What do you think?'

'Let's work, that's what I think.' *I don't want to think.* Katherine reads aloud another of V.V. Sipos' poems.

> *'a girl*
> *dedicates two months*
> *to ritual stripping of flesh*
> *in rites of starvation.*
> *in the third month she'll leave*
> *her core exposed*
> *nowhere to conceal*
> *inadequacies*
> *parental desires*
> *men defiling a jewish grave*
> *fairy penguins flapping oil slicks.'*

'That gives me the shivers. I don't think I'll ever diet again.'

'You never do, Jessie.' Katherine's voice is irritated. 'You know the poem isn't about dieting. It's about being trapped by expectations, hopes, what you want to be.'

Jessie nods. 'I feel trapped sometimes. My dad expects so much and Mum is so weak she always agrees with him. I fight them. Otherwise, I wouldn't be me. I'd be,' she thinks for a moment, 'like that girl. Nowhere.'

*Nowhere. I don't want to be nowhere. That's where I feel I am. I have to talk to Mum. I have to.*

They finish their work just as Jessie's father speeds up the drive. Rachel opens the front door. 'Your dad's here,' she calls out.

'Coming. Is he still having fun with his new toy? I mean his car.' Jessie doesn't stop for an answer as she grabs her books and bag. 'He hates waiting.'

Katherine's mother chats to Jessie's dad through the car window until Jessie appears. 'Thanks a lot for letting me stay. I appreciate it.' Jessie climbs into the front seat. 'And Katherine, thanks. You're a real friend.'

There is waving and shouting goodbyes as the car disappears down the road into the last light of the day. Katherine turns to face her mother. 'Can we talk, Mum? On the back verandah?'

'Yes. I need to talk to you and Rachel, too. Your father is phoning tonight.'

Rachel follows them. The familiarity of the verandah is comforting as evening settles over the house and the ghost gums and on the butterflies flitting among their mother's marigolds and roses. The wicker from the cane chairs is fraying at the edges. Katherine's mother takes out the shears she always carries in her apron pocket and cuts off the bits and pieces. 'That is better.' Reclining into the worn cushions, she waits until her daughters sit down. 'Katherine, can we speak about your father first?'

'Why does he have to call us? ' Rachel punches a cushion. 'There's something wrong with this. It's too lumpy.'

'Don't kill the cushion, Rachel.' Katherine stands up and leans against the railing.

Their mother presses her fingers against her lips. She looks out towards the trees. 'I have been hanging birdseed moulds on the trees, and the rosellas have been pecking at them. Your Nonna always throws bread onto the lawn for the birds, but it is not good for them. Seeds are better.' Then she focuses on the girls. 'When he phones, I will speak to him, then you girls must talk.'

'I don't want to, Mum.' Rachel hesitates, holding her cushion against her stomach. 'It's too difficult. It took me a long time but I've finally worked it out. I don't want those old feelings again.'

Her mother doesn't argue. 'If that is your decision, I will tell him. And what do you want Katherine?'

*I haven't worked out anything. I don't know what I want, what feelings I have. I know I'm angry at you, Mum. But him? Who is he?*

Rachel interrupts. 'He just left us, Katherine, when you got burnt.' Her eyes furrow with incomprehension. 'How could he just have left?'

*I don't know what happened. Do I want to know? Do I want to see him? I don't want to think about him now. It's too hard now. Later, Mum.* Katherine runs her hand against the peeling railing. 'This needs painting.' White paint fragments scatter onto the floorboards. Katherine glances at her mother. *I've got to talk to you, Mum. How can I even start? Will you listen?* Images of the poet afraid to read his work, the girl stripping her body, shuffle inside her head. Katherine forces the images aside. *I've got to tell you, Mum. I have to. I'm not hiding.* 'You know,' she hesitates, 'about William?'

'Yes.' Her mother stiffens.

Katherine's quiet.

Her mother breaks the silence. 'Yes.'

'I thought William liked me.'

'Liked you? How? Did he?' Her mother's accent sharpens.

'Did he?' Katherine repeats her mother's question.

'Did he ...' her mother stammers, 'do ... anything?'

'Do anything?' *That's such a peculiar question.* 'What?' Katherine stares at her mother, trying to understand. Then she recognises something in her eyes.

A look she has when she talks about Katherine's father, about men who are not Grandpapa. An accusing look. Katherine feels the blood rush into her head and she's hot like burning. *Do you mean did he kiss me? Did he press his lips onto mine? Put his tongue down my throat? Hold my breasts, one without a nipple? Did he screw me?* She jolts at the ugliness of her thoughts. She didn't know she was so angry. *Do you think he did that, Mum? He didn't. He doesn't even want to touch me. Who'd want to?* 'No, William thinks I'm ...' she bites her lip, '... ugly. He doesn't want me.'

Her mother's face becomes pale and her eyes fragile. 'That is untrue. Katherine, you are ...'

'Beautiful, I know. You've told me that since I've been little. I'm beautiful. It's just that no one else sees it.' Lifting up her hair, she exposes the heavy scarring reaching down the side of her face and neck, vanishing under her T-shirt. 'You told William about my scars, my face. Why, Mum? Why?'

'I did not. I cannot remember telling him.'

Rachel looks at her mother. 'You did, Mum.'

Katherine moves next to her sister.

'Maybe I did then, but the burns are part of you, Katherine and ...' Searching for an explanation, she looks pleadingly at her daughters.

'Not all men are my father, you know. Was he that bad anyway? What did you do to make him leave?' Katherine turns her back on her mother, leaning over the peeling railing. 'I don't know if I believe he was that bad.'

'He left us. He hurt Mum.' Rachel stands up. 'And me.'

'I want to protect you, that is all. Katherine, you are being unfair.' Her mother hesitates. 'And cruel.'

Spinning around, Katherine protests. 'Cruel? Mum, you don't want me to go out with William or anyone else, so you made him see my scars. How could you? You're always saying I'm normal, like everyone else. Well, you showed me that I'm not.'

'You are normal, better than normal. You do not understand.'

'But I do. I want the operations so that I can try to look like everyone else. You don't want me to, do you?'

'That is not true.'

'Stop it, Katherine.' Rachel grabs her sister's arm, but Katherine can't stop.

'You want me to be your little girl forever.' Katherine's shouting. 'Your protection's choking me. I'm grown up. Next month I'll be eighteen. I won't even be allowed into the kids' ward any more. I'll be having my operations as an adult, Mum. An adult.'

'Being an adult does not mean you are safe. Look at me. Look at all the mistakes I have made. I do not want that for you. I love you so much. These operations will not change you.'

'They will, Mum. They will.'

Katherine runs down the wooden steps into the garden. It's dark. She looks up at the sky. The last rays of sun have been replaced by an incomplete moon. *I feel cruel. I love you so much, too, but it's not enough. It's not enough.*

Katherine bends to smell the roses and sees thorns. *Is that what life's about? Does everything always hurt?* She stands still, looking at the roses as if they'll give her answers. A plain brown butterfly flutters onto a petal.

There is quiet. Katherine alone in the night. Her mother and sister are together on the verandah.

Suddenly, her mother's voice startles Katherine. It seems to shriek through the flowerbeds and night stillness. '*Telefono. Telefono.* It is him.'

*Telephone? Him? What do you want from me, Mama? Everything hurts. Hurts.* Katherine leaves the brown butterfly and the garden with its roses and scents, climbs the wooden steps onto the verandah, avoids her mother's look and slides the back door open. *I'm going to tell my father that I'll see him.*

## CHAPTER FIFTEEN

Lunchtime on the hill is windy. 'Looks like autumn's arrived. We're going to have to move to the back of the Science block soon.' Julia wraps her sweater around herself.

There have been exams all week. Katherine's last exam is today, but others still have History and Geography to do. This afternoon's Maths exam dominates the conversation — questions, study notes, timetables. There is a nervousness in the talk. Even Liz worries about the questions rather than her campaigns — 'Free Whales', 'No Experiments on Animals', 'Save the Rainforests'. During the next holidays Liz is joining an expedition into the Daintree Rainforest. She's protesting against another four-wheel drive track being hacked through the forest.

'Got to do well in these exams. There's next year too. It's pretty hard,' Liz says.

'We're all doing it.'

'I just have to make it into the course, Katherine.'

'And let me guess. What course could that be?'

'Very funny. You know it's Environmental Science.'

'You'll get in, if you want it enough. If it's important enough.'

'It is.' Liz's voice is serious.

Katherine nods. *You're like me, aren't you? You have your dreams and so do I. I just have to make it into Medicine. That's my mission. Mission Impossible.* Katherine listens to her friends sharing their aspirations and inadequacies. *I hope it's not impossible. I like you, Liz. I like you, Jessie. I like all of you. No frightened poets here.*

They move reluctantly to the examination hall when the bell rings. 'You'll do well, Liz.'

'So will you.'

*We'll all be all right. I'm not afraid.*

Katherine smiles as they march like soldiers in line, down aisles. She doesn't smile when they have to break formation to sit at solitary desks. She touches the wooden desk, then looks behind at Liz, who mouths 'good luck' to her. Teachers' instructions force her to pay attention. Exam booklets are placed face down on desktops, pencils sharpened, pens checked, the commencement time marked in black ink on the whiteboard. 'Turn your booklets over. You may start.'

For a moment Katherine stares at the whiteboard, the girls' heads bent down in front of her, the teacher surveying the hall. Opening the exam paper, she picks up her pen and writes her name on the top of the page. She grits her teeth. *I'm not afraid.*

One hour. Two students leave the examination hall. *How could they have finished already?* She looks sideways at Jessie, who's calculating answers on scrap paper. *Concentrate. Another two hours to go.* Touching her lips, she feels their wind-chafed dryness. Katherine takes a boiled sweet out of her pocket, licks it, rubs the sweet over her lips, then sucks it. They're allowed sweets for stamina. She focuses on the paper. Taking a breath, she starts working again. Time becomes irrelevant as problems are studied, calculated, resolved until ... last question. She puts down her pen. Finished. The clock shows ten minutes to go. She checks her answers until the teacher's announcement. 'Pens and pencils down.'

Katherine is in the queue of students who shuffle quietly towards the front desk. She hands in her paper. Outside the examination hall there's relief as they carry out the postmortem. 'Tough paper.' 'Glad that's over.' 'I didn't know the answer to question three.'

'Have to return a book. See you later.' Katherine heads towards the library, chats to the librarian as she hands back the book. Gusts of wind buffet her as she makes her way out of the school grounds, towards the bus shelter. The usual crowd isn't there, just a few stragglers waiting for the late bus. *Hope I don't have to wait for long.* Peering down the road, she imagines she sees a phantom bus. *No bus. I bet it won't be here for ages.* As she sits down next to an old lady on the bench seat, she notices some students standing on the other side of the shelter. She shivers. William is with them, his hands in his pocket, his tie undone, his brown hair cut short and close to his head. She looks down. *William, please don't see me. Hurry up, bus. God, he's seen me. Maybe he hasn't. He has. Okay, okay. What'll I do? I just don't feel like talking to him after the other night. Ignore him. That's it.* She pretends to tie her shoelace, elbowing the old lady on the seat. 'Sorry. Sorry,' she apologises as she stands up, half crashing into someone else waiting at the stop. 'Sorry. Sorry.'

'Hey, watch it. Why don't ...' He stops mid-sentence. Awkwardly, he looks at Katherine. 'It's you.'

*Marc. This is ridiculous.* 'Sorry, I'm bumping into everybody. Must be post-exam nerves.' *What am I saying? I'm not sorry to you for anything.*

He mumbles. 'Our exams aren't until next month.'

'Well, that's my last exam.' *Why am I speaking to you?*

'You caught me off-guard. I didn't expect to see you here.'

'I had things to do at school, so I'm late.' She glances at William, who's looking at them. *You might be useful, Marc. You owe it to me. I'll never forget what you said to me. Hide in a paper bag. Guess what, Marc? I don't have to hide. I'm worth something. I have a body and even a mind.*

'So are you still working at Cafe Smooth? I haven't seen you there for a while.'

*Why are you interested?* 'I work there on and off. Depends.' From the corner of her eye she sees William take his hands out of his pockets.

'It's a good cafe.'

*What are you talking about, Marc? William's still looking. I'll show you that I don't need you, William. You promised to take me surfing and you didn't. You're such a liar.* She moves closer to Marc.

'Would you ... Maybe, you'd like to ... What about coming to the surfboat races? It's just a fun race, on Saturday afternoon. It's the last one of the season. A whole group's going. Looks like the weather will be all right.'

*Are you crazy or something? Has someone put you up to this?* The bus pulls up. She picks up her bag and walks with Marc. As they pass William she smiles at him. 'Hi there, William. Hope the surfing was great.' *Hope it rained and rained.* Then she turns to Marc. 'I'd love to go out with you next Saturday. Let's meet at Cafe Smooth, at around two.' William and his mates follow Katherine and Marc as they board the bus. She sits behind the driver and puts her bag beside her so that the seat is occupied. 'See you Saturday, Marc.'

'Oh, right. So, I'll see you then.'

The bus pulls up at Katherine's stop. She glances back at Marc and William before getting off. *That was so odd. What does Marc want? Hope William is jealous. He's probably not. Anyway, I don't care.*

Yellowing leaves grapple with dark green gums. *I like autumn and it was my last exam today.* She smiles. *Last exam.*

Katherine looks for kookaburras on the way home, but only sees two brown-eyed magpies. *Better watch my head.* When she's entered their territory in the past they've dived for her. She's had a few pecks. Spring is the worst, when they're protecting their chicks. *You remind me of Mum. I'll leave you alone,* and she runs towards her house.

Panting, she calls out. 'Anyone here? I'm back.'

Rachel slams her bedroom door.

'Are you still not talking to me?'

No answer.

Katherine throws her bag into her room. 'Come on. You're never mad at me for that long.'

'Well, I am now, Katherine.'

'So you ARE talking to me.' Ever since the argument on the back verandah, Rachel has ignored Katherine. 'I'm free. No more exams. What about a drive?'

Rachel emerges from her bedroom. 'How are you going to get to the Bronze Medallion training tomorrow?'

'You're giving me a lift.'

'Maybe I will and maybe I won't.'

Their mother arrives carrying pizza. 'Dinner is here. Not as good as what I make, but half ham and pineapple, half chicken.' Katherine likes ham and pineapple and Rachel likes the other. 'Work has been busy with new people and I am late. So it is take-away pizza tonight.'

'I'll make the salad, Mum.' Rachel is already in the kitchen.

Katherine watches her mother put the pizza on the dining room table and place paper serviettes beside three large plates. *I hate being angry at you, Mum.* Looking up, her mother brushes aside hair that has escaped from her bun. Her cheeks are slightly flushed.

'Are you tired, Mum?'

'Yes, I am tired.'

Katherine gets three glasses and a jug of water. The family is quiet as they tear the pizza slices apart. 'Salad, please,' Katherine asks.

Her mother hands her the bowl. 'Now that you have no more exam pressures I must talk to you, Katherine.' She folds the paper serviette thoughtfully. 'I am sorry if I did the wrong thing with William.' Then she straightens the serviette, giving herself time to think. 'You and Rachel do not know so much about men. You have to be careful.'

'Mum, it's normal to go out.'

'Of course it is. That is why you went to the dance.'

'Yes, but you can't expect me to just go to a dance and that's it. It's normal that I'll go out with William or someone else afterwards.'

'I am just worried.'

'Well, don't be.' Katherine shakes her head. *I know you want to protect me but ...* 'It's time to let go, Mum.'

'Katherine, you do not know everything.'

*And neither do you, Mum.* 'You can't cross-examine everyone who takes me out.'

'Is that what I do?' She looks at Rachel.

'Well, yes, Mum.'

'I do not want that.' She takes the paper serviette and wipes her hands. 'I am sorry. Will you accept my sorry.'

Katherine is silent, looks at her mother, then nods.

Rachel carries the plates to the sink and turns on the kettle. She takes out two mugs and her mother's sea-green cup.

Their mother takes a deep breath. 'There is something else. Your father. Will you see him?'

Rachel shakes her head.

Katherine answers slowly. 'Maybe. I've got questions.'

'He can't tell you anything,' Rachel retorts.

'Rachel, I need to work out some things. I want to see him.' *You're pressuring me. Let me think about it, decide. Leave me alone.*

Her mother cups her hands around her sea-green mug. 'I do not know.'

Rachel stares at her sister. 'Well, I don't like it.'

*   *   *

There are six units on each floor. They're on the third floor. From their lounge room window they can see other blocks of units that look exactly the same as theirs. The hallway frightens Rachel with its graffiti and smell of urine. People come to clean it, but the next day it is the same. There are scary people living next door who scream at each other late in the night, but the yard is beautiful with pink oleander trees and a soft green lawn.

'We will not be living here for long.' But she's told Rachel that many times. 'We will have a pretty house soon.'

It had been nearly a year since their mother left their home and their father. He'd been drinking and swearing. Her mother had packed the cooler with sandwiches, fruit, drinks, milk for Katherine's bottle. Her old car was filled to overflowing with clothes, pillows, blankets and the portable TV. The children like watching television when big, yellow teddies run around in their checked shirts. Rachel has her own yellow teddy which she cuddles when she goes to sleep.

They fled from their house in the suburbs — leaving friends, school, familiar shopkeepers, the local Catholic church with the cemetery attached. They didn't have much money and nowhere to go. In the inner city the welfare worker was kind. The emergency accommodation would only be temporary, she'd said.

Later their father came to find them and banged on their door and frightened them. Rachel and Katherine *hid behind their mother. He said he wouldn't pay any money and that he'd see the children when and how he wanted.*

*The welfare worker visits and talks to their mother in the yard. Seven-year-old Rachel is running after Katherine, who is giggling. The gardener working near the oleanders has piled the green garden leaves and clippings in the square, red-brick pit. He throws firelighters and petrol into the leaves because they're still too green. Striking a match, the garden refuse catches alight quickly. He waits until the fire is well established before going to collect the other bundles of clippings to add onto the fire. Petrol pools on top of the uneven red bricks that encase the pit.*

*Katherine's dummy drops onto the grass near the pink oleanders. She bends to pick it up and turns to her sister, who's calling her.*

*Rachel sings. 'Katherine is a bell. Ding, ding, Katie, Kate.'*

*'Rachey,' the baby voice gurgles, then she runs towards the pretty red and yellow flames near the oleanders. 'Rachey. Pretty, pretty. Rachey.'*

*Screaming. Screaming. Scream ...*

*'Katie. Katie.' Rachel runs to get her mother. Then the mother's running, the gardener's running, the welfare worker's running. Rachel stands still on the lawn, crying.*

# CHAPTER SIXTEEN

The Patrol Captain calls out. 'Go.' Sand scatters madly from under bare feet as racers charge across the beach towards the surf. Red- and yellow-quartered caps disappear between plunging waves as they splash furiously out to sea. Conditions are windy, with the waves coming in quick succession. Katherine struggles against a dumper with its tremendous force. She loses control as it throws her against the underwater sand bank. She sees another swimmer tumble too, but Katherine recovers quickly. She looks out towards the horizon. Her arm is free since the graft and with the strength of her swimming training, she speeds towards the coloured buoys. She makes it past the breaking waves, racing towards them. Three other swimmers are with her. Her arms ache as she splashes around the buoys, then she heads back towards the beach. Quickly assessing the waves, she catches a big one that carries her past two other racers. Her feet hit sand and then she runs as fast as she can through the shallow water, tearing from the water onto the sand, sprinting to the finish line between the two flags. As she gasps for breath, the Patrol Captain calls out, 'Second. Good one, Katherine.'

She looks towards the pool, imagining herself standing on the blocks. Waiting for the starter gun. The anticipation, the tension, the dreams. *Do I miss it? The team-mates? The repetitive laps, up and down, up and down. The coach? No.*

Surf racing is quick — pounding arms and legs, splashing, diving, catching waves, body surfing. Surf racing is smart — understanding surf conditions, weather, wave formations, tides, currents. Surf racing has a purpose — training lifesavers to keep beaches safe.

The Patrol Captain addresses Katherine as everyone packs up flags, the rescue reel, the equipment. 'Can I talk to you afterwards? At the clubhouse.'

She glances at the plain brick building that holds the Club's boats, surf skis, boards, rescue equipment. She thinks of her swimming coach and instinctively covers her arms and shoulders with her towel. The Patrol Captain is occupied already, checking equipment and procedures.

At the clubhouse, the surf patrol swimmers jostle each other teasingly. There's discussion in the locker room about training for the summer Surf-lifesaving Championships. Katherine waits in the games room for the Patrol Captain, who is talking to a boy. When he notices her, he waves. 'Just a minute, Katherine. I have to tell my son something.'

Katherine pulls her T-shirt over her wet costume while she waits for him to finish. His hands move with his words as though they are part of his speech, reminding Katherine of her mother. There is something big in his movements, even though he's a short, stocky man. He tousles the boy's hair before sending him to the change rooms.

'Thanks for waiting, Katherine.' He runs his stubby fingers through sun-bleached hair. 'I can see you're a good swimmer, but I think you've got a bit more than that in you. You've got a feel for the surf.' Rubbing his chin, he speaks seriously. 'I'm training a team for the Rescue and Resuscitation Championships. It's tough. A six-person team. A rescue is simulated. It's got to be fast and technically professional, with a beltman, reel team, lifesaving techniques in the water and on the beach.' He stops. 'There's a lot to it. Are you interested?'

'I'm interested.' She hesitates. 'But I have to have some surgery this year. I won't be able to swim really until next year. I can only train on and off for now.'

He thinks for a moment. 'You have to do the theory first, anyway, for your Bronze Medallion. You have to learn how to keep someone alive. There's plenty to learn. If you're not ready for this year's competition, there's next year. The Surf-lifesaving Association is more than a sport.'

She smiles. 'I'm coming to see the surfboat races this Saturday.'

'Good, I'll be there too.' He nods. 'So you'll train with us until the surgery, and start the theory. When you're ready you can join the team.'

'Yes. I'd like that.'

Pleased with her answer, the Patrol Captain puts his hand on her shoulder with its grafts and scars. Surprised, she doesn't jump back but just looks at his stubby fingers. *Can't you see my burns? Does it matter?*

'I'll see you on Saturday.' Then he pats her on the back with a strong, firm hand, *like a father.* 'You'll be a great lifesaver. You're a good kid. A good girl.' Warmth filters through her mind as she leaves the clubhouse. *Good girl.* The words ignite memory. *Did my mother say that to me? My grandpapa? My father? Daddy?* All of a sudden she shivers. *I want to be a good girl, Daddy's good girl. I want the Professor, Mr Roberts, the Patrol Captain to think I'm a good girl. Even Jessie's dad. I want my dad to think that about me.*

Katherine heads for the car park steps. Rachel's meeting her there. 'Thanks for coming to collect me. I know you didn't want to. I'm going to like surf-lifesaving.'

Rachel's voice is sharp. 'Great.'

'Come on, Rachel. Don't be angry.'

'What do you expect? I haven't forgotten what happened the other night.' She refuses to look at Katherine. 'And I know you're going to see *him*.'

'Come on. I'm not doing this against you and Mum. How could I? I couldn't stand it without you. I respect your decision not to see him. All I'm asking is for you to respect mine.'

Rachel shakes her head as they walk towards the car.

'I have to ask him about things. I need some answers, that's all. Maybe I won't see him again afterwards. Maybe I will. It has to be my choice. I can't just do what you and Mum say any more. Please understand.'

'You try to understand. Mum has done everything for us. He hurt her. He'll just hurt you too. We don't need him. Not now.'

'I've got to find that out for myself.' They get into the car. 'Please. I don't want to argue. Rachel, smile, will you? Do you want to come to the surfboat race on Saturday?'

No answer.

'You've got to start speaking to me again because it's ...' Katherine's voice falters, 'it's hard without you. Please, Rachel. Please.'

'You're so stubborn.' Rachel looks at her sister for a moment. 'It's hard for me too.' She hesitates. 'All right, but I still don't approve.'

'I don't expect you to.'

The tension between them eases as Rachel drives, concentrating on gears and pedals.

'The car sounds great,' Katherine exaggerates, then starts explaining surf-lifesaving. 'It's better than competition swimming. You patrol the beach and save people's lives. You need to get a Bronze Medallion to patrol, which I don't know much about yet. And there's the greatest competitions like Beach Flags, which sounds boring, but it's not. It's wild, with everyone diving into the sand and grabbing for a baton. There are belt races, beach sprints, relays, board riding, surf-ski races. I really want to try that. I'll get to paddle on a surf ski right over the waves and there's the ironwoman challenge ...'

'Stop, stop.' Rachel throws her hands in the air. 'You're overloading my brain. If you tell me one more thing I won't come with you on Saturday.'

'Hey, keep your hands on the wheel or you'll kill us.'

'Frightened you, didn't I?' Rachel smiles as she takes control of the steering wheel again. 'Don't worry, I'm an excellent driver.'

'That's what you think.' Katherine laughs. 'But about surf-lifesaving ...'

'I'm warning you, if you don't want an accident, let's get onto something else.'

'All right.' Katherine laughs again. 'I've got interesting gossip. Do you remember Marc?'

'How could I forget him? Revolting.'

'Well, you won't believe this.' Katherine pauses for effect. 'Marc is the one taking us to the Saturday surfboat races.'

'You're kidding!'

'I know it's crazy. Maybe I should stand him up. Should I?'

'Why are you bothering to go with him?'

'It's to do with William.' Her eyes light up. 'And Marc as well.'

'Now this is interesting.'

'I bet you thought William was in love with surfboard riding and that's all? Wrong. Can you believe that I'm in the middle of a love triangle?'

'No, I can't.'

'Well, I am.' Katherine gives Rachel a seductive look. 'Actually, Marc's been trying to meet me in Cafe Smooth and on the bus. He's even tried to get friends to plead his case because he is so desperate for me.' Katherine yawns. 'It's just exhausting chasing him away. Now, Marc is in real trouble because of William, who's the main threat in the battle to win the heart of Beauty. I'm Beauty, if you haven't worked it out yet.'

'You're giving me a big beauty of a story, Katherine.' Rachel pretends to elbow her sister.

'Just listen. It gets sexy now.'

'I can't wait.'

'William, the brooding surfer, has to decide between me or his surfboard. He just loves that surfboard, all smooth and wet. William slides his half-naked muscular body over the smooth board. His body shimmers in the hot sun.'

'But it's autumn. Nearly winter!'

'Shush. William presses his massive groin against the wax, becoming firm and rigid like the board itself. Riding the big, protruding waves, he pushes hard, torpedoing ahead.'

'This is disgusting.' Rachel's laughing.

'Disgusting and dangerous. The route of love with all its twists and turns.'

They're both laughing now and Katherine continues on 'an orgy of rides and slides'. Rachel pulls up in the drive, switches off the ignition and the lights. Katherine is trying to open the car door in between bursts of laughter.

'Hold on, Katherine. Stop laughing.' Rachel waits until they both calm down. 'I still don't understand why you're going anywhere with Marc, but I don't care really.'

'I told you. It's the love triangle.'

'Be serious, Katherine.'

Katherine tries to interrupt.

'Can you listen? Katherine, listen. This is important to me. To us.'

'What is it?'

'I don't care about Marc, but I care about ...' She looks at her sister. 'I don't want him ... you know, our father ... to come between us.'

Katherine shakes her head.

'If he came between us, it ...'

'Rachel, I promise he won't. He can't.' She touches Rachel's hand. 'No one ever will.'

Katherine has already had several appointments with the Professor. He has ordered some pathology tests in preparation for the surgery. On Saturday morning Katherine goes to the blood collection centre. She lies in the chair, which welcomes her with its soft, grey leather. Sighing, she extends her arm. It's routine, automatic. The nurse rubs Katherine's arm with alcohol. It's cold. Katherine turns her head away as she always does. The fine needle pierces her vein like a sting. Three vials of blood today. It's always a relief when the nurse removes the needle and Katherine can press the cottonwool against the pierced skin. Sometimes she doesn't press it hard enough and her arm bruises into a blue and purple patch. The nurse puts on a circular Band-Aid.

Katherine is meeting Rachel at Cafe Smooth. She crosses the road to go through the park, one of her favourite walks. Leaves flood the pathways in the last days of autumn. The roses are just stalks and thorns. Their flowers have wilted into pods. *Why am I seeing Marc?* Katherine picks up a white petal, pressing it. *Marc's like a bruise that's sore. I feel like I have to keep pressing it even though I want to stop.* A possum with curious brown eyes stares at her, then scurries up a tree.

Katherine waves at Rachel, who is sitting on one of the director's chairs outside.

'Have you had your blood taken already?'

Katherine drops her bag on the table. 'It was nothing.' *I really don't want to talk about that.* 'I've just got to say hello to the cook first.'

Katherine is back in a few minutes.

'That was quick.'

'Quick? Right.' Katherine drags out another director's chair, then stares distractedly along the footpath.

'The dental surgery was that busy this morning. It was hard to get away. So these boat races had better be fun.'

Katherine doesn't answer.

'Are you listening?'

'What? Listening? Sure I am.' *Why am I meeting Marc? I'm pathetic, going out with him after what he called me.* 'This could be a mistake.'

'It's a bit late to tell me now. Anyway, I thought Marc was desperately in love with you?'

'Very funny.' *I don't want to go.*

'This cappuccino is terrific. Really creamy. Do you want one?'

Katherine looks around nervously. 'Does this black top look okay? Oh, it doesn't matter anyway, it's only that idiot Marc.'

'I take it that you don't want a cappuccino?' Rachel bangs the table lightly. 'Can you hear me? If you've changed your mind about this afternoon we can just tell Marc to get lost. Or do you want to leave? We can go.'

Just as Rachel says that, Marc appears. He's wearing a Manchester United cap, blue jeans and a white jumper. 'Hi. Are you ready to see the races? They should be good.'

Rachel looks questioningly at Katherine. 'Are we going to the surfboat races then?'

*I don't know. This is humiliating.* Katherine gets up. 'I guess so.' They all leave Cafe Smooth together.

Katherine glances at Marc quickly. *You're good looking. I know you don't think I am. Why am I here?* Marc discusses the skills of trying to row against the waves. 'It'll be a rough one because the wind is up.'

They meet some of Marc's crowd at the beach. Rachel sees a girlfriend and she joins them.

'Lots of people here. I'll be in that team next season.' Marc offers to get Katherine a drink before it starts. Katherine and Marc head for the kiosk. They don't talk. She tries to, but it's as though a cork is plugging her throat. She coughs.

'Are you okay?'

*No, I'm not. What am I doing here with you? What am I trying to prove?*

It's Marc who breaks the silence. 'Do you remember that day at the bus stop? At the beginning of the year?'

*How can I forget? You made me cry.*

'You know afterwards Jessie told me off?'

*Jessie? She never said anything to me.*

He coughs too. 'As soon as I said that to you, I knew I was pathetic. I was showing off.' He takes off his football cap and stops. 'Jessie was right. I was ... gutless. I've been trying to get the courage to tell you ever since. I saw what you thought of me at Cafe Smooth that time we met. I went there on purpose to see you.'

*I can't believe this.*

'I don't know why you said you'd come with me today. I thought you'd stand me up.'

*I nearly did.*

'I'm sorry. I hope you can forget I ever said those things that day. They were stupid and untrue. I am sorry. Sometimes, I'm a real jerk.'

'Yes, you are.'

# CHAPTER SEVENTEEN

The surfboat races seem to have marked the end of autumn as winter winds and rains arrive. Jessie and Katherine walk quickly into the school grounds.

'You didn't tell me about it, Jessie.'

'Are you angry?'

'I would've told you not to say anything to Marc.' Buffeted by the growing storm, they start to run. 'Let's get inside.' They hurry up the stairs into school.

'But are you angry?

'He told everyone that no one would ever want me, that I'd have to hide in a paper bag.' Katherine's steps slow down as she stammers. 'Somehow, it doesn't hurt as much since Marc's said he's sorry.' She touches Jessie's arm. 'It doesn't hurt as much since I know you defended me. No, I'm not angry.'

They hear nervous chatter coming out of classrooms.

'Grades and marks today.' Katherine smiles. 'You'll do fine, Jessie.'

'So will you, Katherine.'

The day is strained as windows are closed to stop rain coming inside and as teachers hand back papers. There are arguments from students afraid of their parents' judgements or upset by their own careless errors and unprepared questions. There is excitement too, with high marks and good grades. Liz is ecstatic over a B in Maths. 'My worst subject. Now I'm ready for the rainforest expedition.'

'Rain is right. I don't know about the forest, Liz. How can you go when the weather is like this? How can your parents let you?' Julia's voice is miserable as she throws her D grade Geography paper on a desk.

'I'm not a little kid so they can't stop me, but why would they anyway? They know it's important to me.'

Looking over Jessie's shoulder, Katherine smiles. 'I knew you'd do it. First in Physics. A grades in everything else, except English. B-plus.'

Jessie flourishes her exam papers. 'After Dad sees this he's going to have to back down about Greg.'

'Greg. Greg. Even first in Physics is just an excuse to go out with him. Your hormones are out of control.' Katherine recites, 'Greg. Greg. "What's in a name? That which we call a rose, by any other word would smell as sweet."'

Jessie pretends to hit her. 'Ha. Ha. So how did you go in English?'

'Not bad. Eighteen out of twenty for my *Romeo and Juliet* essay. A.'

'Who's got the name of a rose now? Mr Roberts?'

'That's a piercing observation, Jessie.'

'No, a fragrant, sweet one, I'd say.'

Katherine moans. 'That was awful.'

'You started it, Katherine.'

Everyone is discussing results when Liz interrupts. 'Guess what?' No one stops until Liz is shouting. 'Are you listening? Party. Do you want to hear? Party.'

Conversations end. Partying is interesting business. 'My parents said that if I passed everything I could have an end of term party.' Now Liz has everyone's attention.

'You have terrific parents.' 'When?' 'What time?' 'Casual?'

'Is it a tofu party?' Jessie teases. 'Oh yes, and I can wear my slinky black VINYL skirt.'

'You'll be sexy as well as saving an animal, so what are you complaining about? And we might have some chilli sauce for the tofu.'

'Hey, who told you about the tofu?'

Liz ignores Jessie's question. 'The party's next Saturday. Eight o'clock and definitely casual. Everyone's invited.'

They play around, teasing each other, joking, letting the pressure of the past weeks disperse into talk of Liz's party and the holidays. By the time the last bell of the day rings, the rain is pelting down. Some girls linger in classrooms, hoping it will ease. Others brave the weather. Cars line the road, disrupting traffic as parents wait for their daughters. Umbrellas buckle as some of the girls make a dash for the bus shelter.

It's late by the time Katherine fights her way home. She's cold. *Heater, heater.* Fumbling with controls, she switches it on. *Hot shower. I can't wait.* As she opens the bathroom door, the vitreous green bathtub seems to stare at her. Katherine always shudders when she sees it. She never has a bath. Rachel has endlessly tried to explain the luxury of soaking in warm, steamy water on a cold, miserable day. She's never persuaded her. Katherine has stopped repeating to her, 'I'm afraid of the hot water.' 'I'm afraid of the bathtub, of not being able to get out.' She can't explain her vague memories of stainless bathtubs and burnt skin, doctors and nurses. She turns on the shower until watery mist fogs the bathroom and is seeping under the door and through the house.

'Lovely and warm in here.' Their mother strips off her raincoat and carries it to the laundry. She asks Rachel to put her umbrella on the verandah, then calls out to Katherine. '*Bambina*, how did you do in your exams?'

Katherine emerges from the bedroom in her warm navy tracksuit. 'Fantastic. Terrific. But what can you expect?'

'There was so much hard rock music coming from your bedroom I was not sure, Katherine.'

Rachel shakes her head. 'How are we going to live with her now? She'll be showing off all night and all day, if I know Katherine.'

'Will not. I can't help it if I'm a ...' she twirls around in a pirouette, 'genius.'

'In your own mind.'

'Obviously I don't get appreciation from my very own family.'

'You are appreciated.' Her mother smiles. 'So what marks did you get?'

The gas heater radiates comfort through the lounge room, making the room intimate. The wind shaking the branches of the gums outside seems distant. They look through exam papers until there's nothing more to say. Discussion turns to the events of the day. 'Liz is having a party. Rachel, you're invited.'

'That will be nice, to go together.' Their mother smiles as she listens to Rachel and Katherine talk about what to wear and who is going. Only when they've finished does her expression become more serious. 'Katherine.' She leans forward. 'The Professor's receptionist rang today.' Her voice is strained. 'Your operation has been scheduled. The Professor wants to see us next week.'

Katherine shivers.

'Are you cold?'

'No, Mum.' *Excited, nervous, happy. I'm here with you and Rachel. At school I have Jessie. And on*

*Saturday, Liz is having a party. It's been a great day. And now there's the new operations. I want them. I'm happy, Mum.*

After dinner, when the girls are washing the dishes, their mother can't wait any longer. She pours filter coffee into her sea-green cup and carries it to the lounge chair. Placing it on the small table, she glances at her daughters before lifting the receiver to seek reassurance from halfway across the world. 'Katherine has done very well, Mama, in her exams ... The operations will mean missing a lot of school, but she should have it done. *Si, si*, yes, she will have to catch up on her studies. Maybe she will do another semester at school ... You will see her at Christmas looking even better ... Katherine will love the knitted bedjacket you made for her to wear in hospital.'

Katherine calls out, 'I'm not wearing a knitted bedjacket.'

'Do you want to speak to her? ... Katherine, you can finish the dishes later. It's your nonna.'

Taking the receiver, Katherine whispers to her mother, 'I definitely won't wear that bedjacket!'

Her grandmother is interested in her school grades and the surf racing and the operations. Grandpapa chats for a while. Then Rachel talks before handing back the receiver to their mother, who has so much to say and so much to hear.

The last days of term are filled with tidying desks, making holiday plans, returning library books. For the last English classes, Mr Roberts hires the video *Tom and Viv* about the life of T.S. Eliot and his wife Vivian Haigh-Wood. 'If you thought V.V. Sipos's poetry shows indecision, then you haven't read T.S. Eliot. I'm looking forward to a few exciting discussions about his poetry next term.'

'Sure.' Jessie nudges Katherine. 'Mr Roberts is always excited, but I'm more excited that T.S. Eliot is the last poet we're studying for the year.'

'Come on, Jessie. It'll be interesting.' They settle into seats in the audiovisual room.

Sprawling country homes and green English pastures splash the affluence of the British upper class across the screen. So different to grey-brown bush and wild surf. Katherine is fascinated by Viv, who's wonderful, crazy sometimes, with a wild intellectual eccentricity that challenges society's rules. Viv falls in love with T.S. Eliot, who is conservative, inflexible, doesn't smile. Katherine elbows Jessie. 'Why does she love him?'

'She's in love with his poetry, not him, if you ask me. Now shush, or we'll miss the next part.'

The film disturbs Katherine. Eliot's increasing rigidity makes him incapable of sympathising with Viv's moods. But he uses Viv's creativity to write his poetry. In the end his oppression drives her to insanity and he commits her to a sanatorium.

'That was terrible. Is that what men can do to you?'

'Men like him. But look at Greg. He's ...'

'Sensitive, kind, sexy. Please, Jessie, can we leave Greg out of this for once?'

'No, because there are lots of guys like Greg. It's ridiculous to say all men are like Eliot in that film. They're not. Otherwise why are we always talking about them, wanting to go out with them? You like William.'

'Well, that ruins your argument, doesn't it?'

'No. You mightn't like William any more, but why are you coming to Liz's party? Is it only to be with the girls?'

'Yes.'

'I don't believe you.'

*Me neither. It's all confusing.* 'Sorry, Jessie. That film has got into me.' *What's wrong with me?* 'So I'll see you on Saturday night? With Greg?' *My father rang. That's what's wrong with me. I'm meeting him tomorrow.*

'See you at the party.'


Saturday. Katherine waits until Rachel's left for the dental surgery. Only then does she get ready to leave. 'Mum, I've got some casual work at Cafe Smooth today.'

'It is very bad weather. Do you want me to drive you?'

'No, Mum. It'll be all right. I'm meeting ... umm ... some girlfriends on the way.' Katherine hurries out of the front door before her mother can ask her anything else. *I hate lying to you, Mum.*

*What else can I do?* The rain has stopped so Katherine detours along the bush track. At first she walks slowly between the wattle trees with their spindly branches and smooth green bark. They've lost their summer flowers and their leaves seem dark and barren. She grabs at the narrow leaves then kicks aside branches that have been blown onto the muddy track. She starts to walk quickly. *He'll be waiting.* She starts jogging. *I've got to get it over and done with.* Then she's running so fast that mud splashes on her joggers and the trees blur into the background. The stitch in her side forces her to stop. *Damn it, I don't want to stop. I want to run, run,* but she leans against a mountain gum with its rough grey-brown bark, waiting for the pain to subside. *I've got to be calm. I wish I'd told Mum.* She tears at the peeling bark, exposing its creamy white trunk. *No, I don't.*

As she leaves the bush track to reach the road, she sees the corner milkbar with its sandwich board out the front — 'Open'. It starts to sprinkle rain again, so she hurries towards it. She notices a kookaburra sitting on the powerlines above. *I hope that means good luck. Or are you giving me a warning?* The milkbar smells stale, as if it has been there too long. A reddish-haired man is sitting at a table. He looks up. *Blue eyes, different to mine.*

Standing, he smiles at her. Katherine doesn't smile. *You look like the photographs in that album. Do I recognise you?*

'Katherine. It's been a long time.'

*What will I call you? Dad? Father? Papa? No, I'll call you nothing.* 'Hello.'

'Do you want something to drink?'

'Cappuccino, please.'

They sit down at the table. He orders two coffees, then looks at her. 'You've grown up.'

*Yes, I'm grown up. All grown up.* A tingle goes down her spine. Confused, she stares at him. *Why don't you know that I'm grown up?*

'How have things been?'

'All right.' *Really hard.*

'What have you been doing?'

*I don't even know where to start. Do you want to know about yesterday? Last year? Ten years ago?* 'Studying a lot.'

'How's your mother? Rachel?'

'They're all right.' *Mum's doing a fantastic job at work. Rachel's a dental nurse and she's studying to be a dental technician.* Katherine smiles to herself — *and she's great at making braids.*

The coffee arrives. Katherine watches his thin lips on the rim of the bulky white cup. He's a tall, heavyset man. A good-looking man. His hands are big. *You could have protected us, made us feel safe.* He says he's still a geologist and works in the outback, around the Kimberleys, for a mining company. He hasn't been back to Sydney for more than ten years.

She stares at him, trying to recognise who he is, what he means to her life, what she's searching for.

*You don't know anything about me, do you? The Professor knows my burns and that I want to be a doctor. Mr Roberts knows I love literature. Jessie's father knows I'm his daughter's friend. Even the Patrol Captain knows I want to do surf-lifesaving. What do you know?*

'I know it's been a lot of years,' he stammers, 'but I'd like to see you, Katherine. And Rachel.'

'Why did you send me birthday cards?'

He speaks slowly. 'Because you're my daughter.'

*Daughter? I don't know what that feels like. What is it?* 'I don't understand.'

His words are careful, quiet. 'I drank too much when I was with your mother and you girls.' He looks into his coffee cup. 'There's no excuse for it, but there are reasons. I didn't like the city. Having kids. It was too much responsibility. Afterwards there was your accident. I wasn't ready. I'm sorry about things.'

*Sorry? Is that why you're here?* 'Mum had to do everything by herself. You hurt her.'

'Yes. Your mother was young, pretty, clever, a good mother.'

'She's still a good mother. Someone I can trust.' *Not like you. You just left us? You didn't like the city. Having kids. Me being … Am I supposed to say it's okay? Rachel hates you.*

'I'd like to talk to your mother and Rachel, and get to know you.'

*Why? Get to know me? What about all those years before? You left. Mum didn't even have her family here. She had to do everything. There were some friends who helped us. Doctors who did surgery for nothing, but it was Mum ...* 'I don't know.'

'I'd like to make it up to you. I feel bad about what I did.'

*You're joking.* Suddenly, Katherine stands up. *Do you want me to forgive you? Say it's all right? Make it up? Can you ever do that?* She stares at him, trying to recognise what she's been searching for. *Who are you? A stranger.* 'Why didn't you help us? Why? You're my father.'

He shifts uncomfortably on the green vinyl seat. 'Please sit down, Katherine.'

*No, I don't want to.* She watches him squirming. *I want you to squirm. You could have been someone important in our lives.* 'I'm burnt, you know.'

'I know.' He pushes his green vinyl seat away from the table to stand up.

'You say that, but if you really knew, why didn't you stay? It's been hard. Mum and Rachel and I have made it alone. There have been so many operations and the burns ...' Katherine stops breathless, as if she's winded.

'You don't understand, Katherine.'

Pressing her hands against her stomach, she stares at him. 'I do.' *You never visited again after I got out of hospital.* 'I wanted a father.'

'I am your father.'

*I understand now, Rachel. I understand.*

# CHAPTER EIGHTEEN

The music blares through the small, seventies house. People crowd into the rectangular family room which extends from the open kitchen. Katherine looks at her watch for the twentieth time. Eleven o'clock. She leans against the canary-yellow pantry cupboards fashionable in the seventies, but glaringly outdated today. The brightness is oppressive and Katherine turns away from it.

She sees Marc drinking with a few mates. He said hello to her when she arrived, but she hadn't wanted to talk to him. A shiver tingles down her back when she notices William with a girl. Turning away, Katherine looks at Rachel chatting with a group of friends. Rachel spent hours ironing her blue jeans and red top until they were creaseless. This time it'd been Rachel who'd asked, 'Do I look all right?'

Through the glass doors Katherine glimpses Jessie and Greg on the back terrace. Jessie's wearing a thick beige jumper over her black vinyl skirt. The skirt is tight, provocative. Katherine can just see Greg's hand sliding over her hips.

Soft drinks are laid out on the kitchen bench and on a cabinet near the glass doors. Corn chips, hoummos, nuts, salsa, avocado dip are scattered on tables throughout the room. 'Pizzas are coming soon,' Liz announces as she whirlwinds through the room.

The bathroom door is open. The bathtub looks benign, packed with ice and beer cans. 'No glass bottles. I don't want smashed glass everywhere,' Liz had said. Katherine watches some of the guys stumbling across the dance floor.

Pizzas arrive. Vegetarian, cheese and pineapple, anchovies and mushroom, double-cheese pizzas line the bench. Everyone descends into the kitchen, around the bench, grabbing and pushing until Katherine is squeezed like toothpaste into the hallway.

*I want to go.* Jessie's father is driving them home, but Katherine knows that if she phones her mother she'll come now. *You're always there, Mum. No one else has been.* She thinks of the afternoon, meeting her father. It makes her shudder. *When will this party end?*

She's startled when Liz grabs her arm. 'Come on, we're throwing Julia.'

'Throwing Julia? What?' Katherine is dragged into the circle. Even though the rain is beating against the windows, the room is hot and stuffy. Pumping music establishes a hypnotic pulse. Empty beer cans are thrown to the floor as hands are raised. Julia climbs on top of the hands, screaming when there's a dip, screaming when there's a high. Jessie climbs up, her vinyl skirt edging up her thighs. Leaning on a few guys' shoulders, Greg climbs up too, so that three of them rollercoaster over currents of movement.

By the time Liz turns down the music, everyone's sweaty and laughing. Taking a six-pack of beer, Marc and his mates sit on the back terrace. Someone puts on a slow song and dims the lights. Jessie and Greg are hardly moving as they sway in each other's arms. Rachel is dancing with Liz's older brother.

'Do you want to dance?'

Katherine doesn't answer as William takes her hand. There is a faint smell of alcohol on his breath. She can't think. He puts his arms around her and she leans against his chest, shuffling slowly with the music. *What did I expect from my father? What could he have said to me? Sorry? That's not enough.* William is talking to her. *What are you saying? You don't want me. I'm too ugly, aren't I? Are you dancing with me as a joke or is it the alcohol?* He presses her against him. *You're so warm. I wish you cared about me. I wish someone did. Why didn't you ask me out? You promised.* Suddenly she's angry, really angry. She looks into his hazel eyes. *I like the colour of your eyes, but I don't like you.* 'Why didn't you take me surfing?'

'Surfing? Umm . . . it was only . . . for the guys.'

'Why didn't you ask me out somewhere else?'

He shifts uncomfortably. 'I wanted to.'

'No you didn't.' She speaks quietly. 'It's because of my burns.' *That's why my father didn't want me. You're the same.*

He stammers, 'That's unfair.'

'Is it?'

'Yes, Katherine.'

She moves out of his arms.

'I've had to study. There's the surfing too ...'

Katherine shrugs her shoulders. 'Sure.'

'All right. Do you want the truth?'

'Yes.'

'It seemed too ... tough to go out with you. Your life's ... complicated. I wasn't ready.'

Katherine shudders. *Ready? Ready for what? Don't say that. My father wasn't ready. Ready, ready ...*

'I wanted to go out with you.' He gently pulls her back into his arms, and Katherine feels she can't pull away. 'I think you're special. You're smart, interesting and ... okay ... will you go out with me?'

*Go out with you? How can I?* She doesn't answer. Focusing on the music, she's quiet as they move in time with the rhythm. Other couples dance near them, touching each other, holding each other. Jessie and Greg are kissing slowly in the corner. Katherine leans against William's shoulder, grateful that he doesn't speak.

As arranged, Jessie's father arrives to collect them at one in the morning. They run out to the car. 'Don't want Dad to see what's going on inside,' Jessie whispers to Katherine and Rachel as they get into the back seat.

Jessie diverts her father with descriptions of the party until they reach Katherine and Rachel's house. Before driving away he waits until their mother opens the front door and waves.

Rachel drops her handbag into her room then goes to the kitchen to put on the kettle. 'Mum, Katherine. Do you want hot chocolate and biscuits?' Fossicking through the cookie jar, Rachel shakes her head at her sister. 'Someone's eaten all the mint ones.'

Katherine feels too disturbed to go to bed. She slouches into an old armchair next to her mother and sister around the heater. Rachel talks about Liz's brother. 'He's nearly finished his apprenticeship. Plumbing. He asked for my phone number.'

Katherine listens as confidences are shared in the early hours of the morning — the party, friendships, a promise of a promotion for Mum, the operation, dental courses, grandparents visiting — and it feels warm and safe. *I wish I could tell you about my father. He's my secret from you and I hate that. I don't know what he means to me, but he's not part of my life. You are. You're my family.*

Katherine sips her hot chocolate. Winter means that her mother's roses and jasmine, kangaroo paw and birds of paradise are not flowering. *Birds of paradise. Flowers called birds, as though they're flying with their orange wings and blue tail.* Curling up into her chair, Katherine thinks to herself. *I wonder if*

*William likes me?* Getting more comfortable, Katherine nestles into her armchair. *I'm home.*

*Home. Rachel runs and runs around the backyard of her home. Katherine follows her like a mummy, bound up in her elastic suit.*

*Their smart, neat lawn is mowed regularly by government workers from the Department of Housing. On the back verandah there are cuttings from friends' gardens and seedlings growing in small plastic pots waiting to be transferred into soil. 'I have to prepare the garden beds first.' Their mother has already dug trenches along the side fences. Overlooking the back fence, there is bushland. Two eucalyptus trees are inside the backyard fence. Katherine points excitedly to a kookaburra.*

*'We can hang pots of seeds from the trees for the birds, Katherine.'*

*They each have their own room, but Katherine shares with Rachel. She's afraid of the dark and cries if Rachel doesn't sleep with her. After Katherine's accident, they got priority for a cottage from the Department of Housing.*

*'Thank you, Mama. I love this house.' Rachel hugs her mother and Katherine chases the kookaburra.*

The Professor walks towards them as Katherine and her mother enter his rooms. His eyebrows furrow together. 'Come in. Come in.' He points to two chairs, then pulls out his chair from behind the desk. He sits down, shuffles a little in his chair, then carefully begins to explain the procedure of transfer of skin and tissues to the face, neck, shoulders, the cutting out of scars and distortions. Katherine listens to the medical jargon she's heard since she's been a little girl. He speaks softly. 'It will be painful and you have to be prepared.'

Katherine's mother looks at her.

'I am.'

He leans his chin against his hand. He points to a diagram, discussing the details of the procedures. 'Am I being too technical?'

*I don't want to listen to clinical explanations of skin and grafts today.* She looks up at the Professor's framed diagrams of miracles. Her mind wanders, dreaming about putting her hair into a high ponytail like Jessie does.

'The surgery is delicate. Remember, this is only the first stage. Afterwards I'll need to refine the shape and texture. So there'll be a number of operations on the neck, the side of Katherine's face.'

Katherine touches the right side of her face.

He pauses. 'Katherine, I want to be honest. There are no guarantees. You have to be prepared for a rejection of the tissue and imperfect results.'

'I trust you.'

'Please don't. Katherine, I can only promise to do my very best.'

Katherine's mother is quiet as they make their way to the car. Katherine asks her what's wrong.

'Nothing is wrong. I am thinking about the new

operations. It will be easier than when you were a little girl. You are older. You understand more.' She hesitates. 'I hope you will not be disappointed.' She brushes aside her daughter's hair. 'Even if it does work, it may not be as you imagined.'

'Mum, I've had disappointments before.' She puts her arm through her mother's. 'But you've taught me hope. If it doesn't work this time, I'll try again. It will work in the end. I know it will.'

'You are beautiful the way you are.'

Katherine smiles. 'So you keep telling me.' She gets into the car. 'Let's go. Rachel's taking me to the surf clubhouse tonight. Don't want to be late.'

'No, we won't be late.'

Rachel drops Katherine at the clubhouse. 'I'll be back in time to get you.' She's meeting Liz's brother for coffee and she's nervous. Rachel rarely goes out.

'Real loyalty. A date's more important than supporting my training.'

Rachel rolls her eyes.

'Don't be late to pick me up or you'll have to tell me every, disgusting detail of THE DATE.'

'You're ridiculous. As if there will be any details, and they wouldn't be disgusting anyway. It's your mind that's disgusting.'

That sends Katherine off into a peel of laughter as she leaves her sister and heads for the clubhouse. The Patrol Captain is already there, organising fitness programs for his patrol. Katherine watches his hands.

They seem to encompass everyone as he instructs some on techniques, others on surf awareness, everyone on fitness. She waits until he sees her. 'Do you remember that I said I've got to go to hospital? Well, it'll probably be a few months before I can get back here.'

Katherine's thankful that he doesn't ask about her surgery. He just accepts it. 'There's the theory I told you about before. I'll give you a Training Manual tonight. It'll start you on the way to getting your Bronze Medallion. You need it for patrolling the surf and my Rescue and Resuscitation team. You can call it R&R because you're nearly a team member, aren't you?' Smiling, he points to the rowing machine. 'Today, you can train with the others. Fifteen hundred metres on the rower, then the treadmill. Say another fifteen hundred. Then weights. You have to maintain fitness over winter. The open sea isn't a place to begin a "get fit" program. I've seen lifesavers in trouble when they do that. But you won't get into trouble. You know where you're going.'

She straps her feet into the rower. Grabs the wooden handle, then pulls hard, straightening her legs as she jerks it out, bending her knees as the chain contracts. Pulling, straightening, pulling ... *Know where I am going.* The Patrol Captain's words repeat in her mind as she looks ahead. Katherine enjoys the rhythmic movement of her arms pulling, releasing, pulling, releasing. 'One, two, one two, one two,' she counts to herself until she's in a familiar routine and her thoughts are free. *Where am I going?*

## CHAPTER NINETEEN

*Eighteen. How do I feel about it? Grown up? Afraid?* She picks up Pup and hugs him. *Mum wants to give me a party. I just can't have one before the operations.* She looks through the presents she's been given. A CD from Jessie, a wildlife book from Liz, some soaps and bubble bath from other girls. *Nonna and Grandpapa sent me one hundred dollars. I'm going to save that for my holidays.* Looking out of her window she tries to see if there are any buds on the trees. *No, it's still winter. William asked me out for my birthday. He did kiss me once, but if he touches me now, after everything, I don't think I could stand it.* Katherine hugs Pup again. *Don't worry, I'm supposed to be too complicated for William. Complicated? He means my scars. But they're part of me. He'd have to touch them.* She shudders. 'So Pup, you're my only boyfriend after all.' She kisses his patchy head.

'Ready?' Her mother calls out. 'The restaurant is booked for seven-thirty. We do not want to be late and miss the show.'

'Coming.' Katherine throws Pup onto her bed.

'After this show you will not listen to this hard rock any more.'

'Sure, Mum.'

The doorbell rings. 'I'll get it.' Rachel opens the front door. 'Wow!'

'Someone likes you,' the delivery man says as he waits for her to sign.

Rachel looks at the attached note. 'They're not for me.'

'Don't worry. The next one will be.' He whistles as he heads for his truck.

'I don't want the next one.' She hands Katherine the posy of pink roses intertwined with maidenhair fern.

*To Katherine,*
*Happy 18th Birthday*
    *from your father*

Their sweetness makes her shiver. *He's sent me another birthday card. Flowers too.* She puts the flowers into the kitchen sink. 'They're from him.' She doesn't look at her mother.

Her mother walks up beside her. 'The flowers are

pretty.' Her accent softens the words as she speaks. 'Eighteen years old.' She pauses. 'Eighteen years is a lifetime.' Fleetingly she places her hand over Katherine's. 'You make your own decisions now about your life. I will always be there, but it is time.' She glances at Rachel. 'What is important is that we are together.'

'Thank you, Mum.' Katherine kisses her mother.

Rachel taps her watch. 'Come on. We'll be late if you keep standing there.'

Katherine leaves the pink roses in the sink. 'What type of place are we going to anyway?'

'You'll see. Let's just go.'

The restaurant is crowded. Guitars, old LP records, sheet music, 60's music posters, leather gear are plastered over the walls. The waiter's black hair is slicked down with gel except for a wave of hair hanging over his forehead. 'Sexy.' Katherine winks at him. 'Elvis reborn.' The waiter shows them to their seats.

'This is a crazy restaurant, Mum.' Katherine looks at the plastic menu folder. 'But great food. Pasta and pizza. I want ham and pineapple of course.'

As the lemonade is served, their mother takes a bottle of wine out of her bag. 'Your grandfather sent this special wine from the village. *Sciacchetra*. It is sweet. We always had this wine with our evening meal. You will like it.'

'Elvis and wine. That's a pretty wild combination. And I thought you disapproved of alcohol,' Katherine adds jokingly.

'No. It is drinking too much that is bad. This is different and we must celebrate tonight.'

'And I'm the legal age now.' Katherine takes the bottle and calls the waiter over.

It sparkles into their glasses. 'To Katherine,' Rachel toasts as they clink glasses.

Rachel produces a small package wrapped in paper covered in pictures of puppy dogs.

'Pup's into everything, isn't he?' Katherine smiles.

'This is from Mum and me, as well as Pup.'

Katherine opens the card:

*To my daughter Katherine,*
*You were a beautiful baby and you are still beautiful. There have been so many battles to overcome in your life and you have been remarkable. Thank you for being special. You will have a wonderful future.*
*I love you always, Mama*

*To Katherine*
*Now you're eighteen, you're old enough to keep your room TIDY, but more importantly, keep the BATHROOM tidy. You never know who'll see your undies lying on the floor there. It mightn't just be Pup!*
*Apart from that, you're the best sister anyone could have.*
*Love, Rachel*

Slowly Katherine unwraps the puppy-dog paper. 'I want to keep the paper.' Inside, there is a dark-blue velvet box. She strokes the velvet before opening it. Rachel and her mother lean towards Katherine, shutting Elvis and the restaurant out of the moment.

'It's lovely.' She lets the shining gold chain hang from the palm of her hand and holds the finely engraved pendant. Three small diamonds are encrusted in the top of Katherine's initial. 'I love it.' Katherine puts it around her neck. 'I love it.'

Suddenly Elvis the Pelvis blasts onto the floor. 'Love me tender, love me true ...' His crystal-studded white vinyl shirt is unbuttoned nearly to the waist. Tight white pants bulge under his big, black-buckled belt. A girl at the next table screams, 'Elvis, we love you.'

The pianist dressed in black leather gear accompanies Elvis, who pivots wildly around the tables. 'Oooohhh. Come on, sweetheart ... Love you aaalll.'

'Heartbreak Hotel', 'Wooden Heart', 'Suspicious Minds' ... Elvis belts out songs and the audience joins in, singing, cheering. Elvis serenades the girl who screamed out at the start of the show. 'You know that I'll always love you.' He leaves her swooning and turns to Katherine. Taking Katherine's hand he kneels at her feet singing, 'I'll always love you.'

Katherine blushes and her mother blushes with her. Rachel takes out her camera when Elvis sings 'Happy Birthday'. A cake with twinkling candles is brought out by the Elvis-lookalike waiter. The whole audience sings Happy Birthday until Katherine's shaking her head, laughing.

It's one of those nights where everyone joins in the rock and rolling, around tables, singing into the pianist's microphone with Elvis, who is gyrating his sexy hips. At two in the morning, the restaurant finally closes and everyone calls out goodbye as if they're old friends.

The three women walk arm in arm down the street, singing '*since my baby left me ...*' Katherine touches the pendant around her neck. 'I'm happy.'

Katherine shows her friends photographs of the Elvis the Pelvis night.

'Is that really you singing into the microphone, Katherine?' Julia asks.

'You have no idea what a terrific voice I have,' Katherine jokes. 'Actually I think I drank a bit too much *sciacchetra*.'

'What's that?'

'Delicious. Wine, of course.'

'I think Mum drank a bit too much too. She was pretty wild.' Katherine shows her friends a photo of her mother dancing with an Elvis lookalike.

Jessie shakes her head. 'That's unbelievable. Your mother is usually so,' Jessie thinks for a moment, 'responsible.'

*Responsible. She's had to be. But for my birthday, she was young and silly and not responsible. I liked her being young.* 'The Elvis waiter was the unbelievable one. His sideburn fell off. I found it in the salad. I thought it was a caterpillar.'

That starts Julia onto a story about how she found half a worm in her apple, after she'd bitten into it.

'Disgusting.' 'Awful.' 'Julia ate meat, Liz.'

Liz ignores the meat joke and starts a lecture on the importance of earthworms in the soil until the bell interrupts her.

'Saved by the bell,' Jessie whispers to Katherine. Jessie pulls off her jumper. 'The weather's getting better.'

Katherine looks up at the sky. 'No clouds today. I can actually see the sun.'

'I can too.' Jessie smiles as they walk to class.

They are unpacking their bags when a duty monitor speaks to Katherine. 'I've been looking for you. The Senior Coordinator wants you in her office. Now. You know the rotten mood she gets in if she's kept waiting.'

'What's it about, Katherine?' Jessie asks.

Katherine shrugs. 'I don't know.'

The Coordinator's door is half open. Katherine peers inside.

'Hello Katherine. Come in. Come in. How are you?'

'Fine.'

'Good. We've got a lot of things to discuss and prepare. Sit down.' Adjusting her metal-framed glasses, she indicates the other side of her desk. 'I need to write to the Education Department regarding your operations. I will arrange to stagger your exams over a number of terms so that you are not penalised when you miss school later in the year. There are a lot of concessions we can get for students like you. Your mother is ethnic, too, an Italian. That's good, and a sole parent as well. All that helps.' She fills in forms while she speaks. 'Concessions for student with special needs.'

*Special needs?* Katherine jerks forward, scraping the aluminum legs of her chair against the floorboards. *Special needs?*

'All right. Let's begin.' The Coordinator starts reading out questions. 'Name, Age. Address. Mother's name. Language spoken at home. Disability. Katherine, how old were you when the accident occurred?'

*Disability?* 'Three.'

'I need medical records. Who is your current doctor? What hospital? When was the last operation? When are the new operations proposed? Your mother is a sole parent. She's working now? Where is that?'

*Disability? Special needs?*

*Katherine is five, running around in her elastic suit with a piece of soft, yellow foam wedged under her right arm to stop webbing. She doesn't like the 'sausage' and lets it fall to the ground.*

*Her mother picks it up, calling out to Katherine, 'Come here. Come here now.'*

*She doesn't, and her mother has to chase her until Katherine's running. 'Stop Katherine.' But she doesn't, running faster and faster, laughing at the game.*

*Her mother is puffing and red when she catches Katherine. 'You are a naughty girl. This isn't chasings.' But Katherine giggles and blows big kisses.*

*'You are a naughty girl, but I love you so much.' She strokes Katherine's round, flushed cheeks. 'Please be good. Don't throw the sausage away. You upset Mummy. You'll make me cry. Do you want to do that?'*

*Katherine shakes her head. 'No, Mama. No, sausage.'*

*'You need it to get better. You're my special girl and when you wear this it makes you even more special.'*

*Katherine's face scrunches into a frown. 'I don't want to be special, Mama.'*

When the Coordinator finishes her questions and has filled in as many papers as she can, she says to Katherine, 'Go back to class. You shouldn't miss more classes than you have to. You and your mother will have to sign some forms later.'

Katherine stands to leave, then hesitates. 'I'm not, I'm not disabled you know.'

The Coordinator looks up.

'I won't sign anything that says I'm disabled.'

The Coordinator takes off her glasses. 'But you have some difficulties.'

'They're only skin deep,' Katherine answers derisively.

The Coordinator taps the desktop.

Katherine stands with her feet apart and her arms folded.

The Coordinator puts down her papers.

'I won't sign anything that says I'm disabled.' She speaks softly but clearly. 'I've had to go through too much to do that.'

'Well, of course.' The Coordinator hesitates. 'I didn't mean that you are.' She goes faintly red.

'I won't sign.'

The Coordinator looks at the papers on her desk, then starts to flick through them. 'Let me see. Let me see.' She repeats. 'Oh, there's an error.' She looks up at Katherine. 'I can get exemptions under sickness criteria for the operations and recovery period.'

'I won't sign.'

Her voice is more personal. 'Katherine, everyone can apply under that criteria.'

'Not just special students?' Her lips are dry.

'Everyone, Katherine.'

'I don't know.'

'Katherine, you have the right to be given the same consideration as all the other students.' She stumbles over her words. 'I don't regard you as disabled. I apologise.' She stands up from behind her desk and moves towards Katherine. 'I need to make the application so there is a level playing field. You've missed so much school.'

Katherine nods.

The Coordinator walks her to the door.

CHAPTER TWENTY

The next weeks are tense as teachers issue home assignments for the holidays, friends ask questions, Katherine sees the Professor, her mother talks about the new surgery. William's been phoning since the party. They've met a few times at Cafe Smooth with other friends. Katherine feels as though life is on hold until the operations start. She half trains for surf-lifesaving, walks her bush track, postpones her exams. Cafe Smooth promises her regular work, but only next year.

*Surgery, in a few days.*

It's Saturday afternoon when William phones. 'Do you need a break from studying?'

'Yes.'

'Me too. Maybe we can go for a walk, then coffee and cakes afterwards? I know you like cakes, especially chocolate ones.'

That makes Katherine laugh. 'I'd like to, but I have to really put in some extra work before next week and you know … surgery.' *I'm not hiding it any more, not to William or anyone.*

'Does that mean you're not doing any bush walks now?'

'Well, no, but …'

'Fresh air clears the brain. I'd like to see where you go on your walks. Sounds nice.'

'It is.' *But I'm nervous. Another operation. It's what I want, but I'm still nervous. I can't see anyone now, especially not you, William.*

'So can I come over?'

*No.* 'Okay.' She shakes her head as she puts down the receiver. *Why did I say that? I don't want to go out with William.*

'Mum! Mum!' Katherine searches the house. 'Where are you?' She opens the back door and sees her mother digging in the rose garden. 'Mum, I'm going for a walk.'

'*Per favore*, please come here Katherine. I want to show you this. There are buds. Pink and yellow ones.'

Katherine looks at the roses, then bends to smell them. 'They're pretty but no scent, Mum.'

'Too early for scent.' She wipes her hands on her apron, and gets up. 'I have had enough gardening today.'

Katherine bites her lip. 'William's coming over.'

Her mother is quiet for a moment. 'Katherine, I know you talk sometimes with William.' She picks up her garden bucket. 'Come inside. I have to put on the lasagna. Rachel has a late class tonight and she will be hungry when she gets home.' She pauses. 'Would you like William to come for dinner?'

Katherine doesn't answer immediately as they climb up the back steps. 'Thank you, Mum. It means a lot that you asked. But not tonight. Thank you.'

After grabbing a jumper from the pile of clothes thrown onto her chair, Katherine sits on the front steps to wait for William. His old Valiant pulls up outside the house. William gets out, carefully puts on the steering lock, because he's got no car insurance. Can't afford any, he says. He walks in big strides towards the house. *Your eyes look like they're smiling, William. Hazel eyes. I still love them. I can't believe I'm going out with you.*

Hiding a sheepish grin, he gives her a card and a package. 'You have to open the packet first.'

'That's not very polite of me.'

'Be wild and break the rules.'

'Ha. All right. I'll be wild.' She tears the paper wrapping and starts giggling. Inside the wrapping is a porky pig made of milk chocolate with a white chocolate nose and a red ribbon around its neck. 'Is this supposed to be me? I should hit you for that.'

'Please, be kind. You know pigs are intelligent, affectionate and ...'

'Give up, William. But it is cute.' She smiles. 'Very cute. Now, can I open the card?'

'It's an early get well card.'

Katherine opens the bright yellow envelope. Inside is a pig card covered in pigs with curly tails all wrapped in bandages. *Being sick is a curly problem, It needs to be straightened out.*

'That's the worst joke I've read.' Katherine shakes her head. 'Maybe it'll improve inside the card.' She reads the illustrated captions aloud. *'The owner of a pig takes Piggy to the doctor. She says, "My poor pig has lost her voice." The Doctor looks at Piggy and starts fixing her up. "Doctor, what are you rubbing on her?"'* Katherine looks up at William for effect. *'"OINKMENT. OINKMENT!"'*

They both laugh and laugh, and 'oinking' can be heard all the way down to Katherine's bush track.

Katherine is surprised as William identifies trees, plants, flowers and the birds that are part of the bush. 'See that brown butterfly. It's amazing to think that one little butterfly has spread nearly everywhere in the world. I guess you're just got to be persistent.'

Katherine smiles. 'Persistent? Are you talking about the butterfly or you?' *Or me? I feel like a little brown butterfly sometimes. Flapping my wings trying to get somewhere, but the wings are fragile.* 'You know a lot about the bush.'

'My boy scout days.' He gives the boy scout salute. 'I don't admit to being that to everyone. We did a lot of bushcraft and went camping a fair bit. I liked it.' He stops suddenly. 'Did you hear that?'

'What?'

'Shush.' He points to leaves and brush. 'See it?' There's a little pointed nose and big brown eyes peering out of the leaves. 'An echidna. There are the furry spines.'

'I can't believe it. I've never seen one before, except in the zoo.'

'You've probably passed by echnidas before, but you haven't noticed.'

'It's beautiful.'

'Yes, it is.'

Silently they watch the echnida, until it burrows back into the leaves. 'That was special, William.'

He smiles.

'I haven't been to the Falls for ages. Can we go there? It's a bit of a detour.'

'That's fine.'

Katherine isn't sure what they talk about but it feels natural as they walk between the trees, bypassing a huge fallen mountain gum. Making their way across a rickety wooden bridge, they hear water. There is a small clearing which leads to the lookout. Katherine runs towards it. William follows. 'Hey, slow down. What's the hurry?'

They reach the wire fence together. Looking over it, they see the waterfall. Water breaks over the cliff face, plummeting into a rock pool. Swirling foam crashes over rocks and fallen branches until it settles into the stream. Silently they watch the movements of the water. Katherine shivers.

'Are you cold? '

She nods.

'It gets cold in the late afternoon.' He moves closer to her. She keeps staring down at the water crashing into the pool. He puts his arm around her. 'Is that warmer?'

*What are you doing? Take your arm off me. Don't dare touch me. But you gave me a pig. I liked the pig and the card.* 'Yes, it's warmer.'

William touches her hair. 'It's so soft.'

*Don't touch my hair. It's been pulled and dragged over scars. There are burns. Don't you remember? I'm too complicated.*

He starts stroking her hair and she wants to stop him, but, *it feels so warm, comforting,* and Katherine is as weak as though her body is soft Plasticine. She half whispers a protest. *You don't like me, do you?* Her stomach butterflies into knots and yearnings and she murmurs, 'Stop' ... s*top, William, please ... don't stop.*

He turns her face to his.

*You're too close. Don't William. Don't. I'm ugly. You know it. You can see.* Instinctively she raises a hand to hide scars.

He takes her hand, drawing it aside. Breathing slowly, he puts his arms around her. His breath intermingles with hers and gently he kisses her lips, again and again.

\* \* \*

Dinner, family, chatter. Katherine is quiet. She clears the table. Dishes are washed and dried and the evening routine completed. 'I'm tired. I'm going to bed early. Goodnight, Mum. Rachel.'

*I want to dream tonight.*

Katherine opens her window to look out into the evening garden with its shadowy lights and fragrant scents. She puts the chocolate pig next to Pup on the windowsill. The cold of the night air makes her shiver as she takes off her jumper, dragging it over her head. Unbuttoning her blouse slowly, she shivers again. Her jeans slide down her thighs and she rubs the small indentation the button has left on her stomach. Unclipping her bra, she watches the plain white cotton drop to the floor. She rubs the palms of her hands over the silky satin of her pants. Something special she bought herself for her birthday. There is no flannelette nightie or pyjamas tonight.

Goosebumps ripple over her body as she stands in her satin pants looking around her room. There are photographs of her mother, Rachel, Katherine; textbooks piled on her bookshelf; Pup at the window; cream for her scars; her golden necklace on her dressing table; birthday cards displayed; drawers filled with letters, medical appointments, assignments . . .

She puts William's card next to her bed, switches off her side lamp then slides under the warmth of her quilt, letting sleep gradually descend.

\* \* \*

*Hands stroke her wounds, but they don't hurt her. Tingles wander along her spine radiating into her arms and legs. The hands linger over her face and arms, before stroking her long, brown hair. Fingers trace the intricacies of her nakedness, the back of her neck, her back, sides, bellybutton ... making Katherine moan in her sleep. The fingers become soft male lips, brushing over her stomach and breasts like wings of butterflies. A butterfly lands gently on her perfect nipple ...*

*Katherine crushes the quilt between her legs as William's lips rhythmically suck her breasts, as his hands explore her thighs searching down past the quilt, down past the satin. William's fingers discover quilt and satin as Katherine presses herself against them ...*

# CHAPTER TWENTY-ONE

Mum should get her promotion, don't you think? She deserves it.'

'She will, Rachel. Mum can do anything.'

*'Mama can do anything, Rachey.' Katherine lifts her chin up watching their mother organise the tables for the lunch at the Burn Support Group in the Health Centre. Sometimes their mother speaks about Katherine at meetings of the Support Group and they clap her. Sometimes other people speak, but Katherine knows they never clap for other people as loudly as for her mama.*

*While their mother is busy with lunch, Katherine and Rachel play on the swings in the playground attached to the Centre. A boy who can't separate his fingers throws a ball with his left hand to Katherine, who throws it to Rachel, who throws it to a dark-haired girl. The dark-haired girl can't stretch her arm out properly and the ball rolls past her. She starts to cry.*

*'What is wrong, mia cara? Do not cry. It cannot be so bad,' Mama calls to the little girl, leaving the luncheon preparations. She hurries over. 'Do not be upset. It is only a game.' The girl's tears wiggle crookedly down her burnt cheeks and Katherine's mother wipes them gently away. 'I have special pink limonata. Lemonade. Would you like some?' She takes the dark-haired girl's hand and they go to get some pink lemonade. The girl stops crying.*

*'See. Mama can do anything ...' she tells Rachel, who's getting the ball.*

Rachel picks up a magazine from the table. She hands it to Katherine. 'There's a great article on rock bands in here. You can read it in hospital.'

Katherine puts the magazine in her bag. 'The Professor says the operation is going to be long.'

'You'll make it.' Rachel pauses. 'This is what you want, isn't it?'

'Yes.' Katherine puts the 'Good Luck' cards everyone has given her in a pile. 'I can't believe the Coordinator sent me a card. Have a look at this one from Jessie. It's pretty funny.'

Rachel reads the front. *'Aw, c'mon! Cuddly-Wuddly Puppy wants you to cheer up!'*

She opens it.

'*Kinda makes you want to squeeze cuddly-wuddly puppy's little neck until his itsy-witsy button eyes pop off, doesn't it?*' Rachel giggles. 'That is funny.'

'And it reminds me. Come on Pup, into my bag.' Katherine shows Rachel William's piggy card. She doesn't show her the card from their father which says he'll visit her in hospital.

'Ready?' her mother asks Katherine as they begin a routine as familiar as having breakfast, but this morning there is no breakfast.

'Just be prepared. It is a long operation,' her mother says as they drive to the hospital.

'You are beautiful as you are,' her mother says as they wait for admissions.

'Your hair transplants already cover the burning and your hair is pretty,' her mother says as they go to the ward.

'I'll be perfect one day, Mum.'

Tears fill her mother's eyes.

Admission. Hospital. Preparations. Nervousness. No visitors. The Professor, doctors, nurses, procedures. Her mother. Pup. 'Mum, I want this.'

Her mother walks beside her as the bed is rolled along familiar corridors towards the operating theatre. The orderly jokes with Katherine, and her mother hovers as always, protecting her against strangers. The Professor peers over Katherine before the surgery. 'Are you sure? Do you understand?'

'Yes, I'm sure.' Yes, I understand that *I'm afraid*. *Mama, I'm afraid*. She stretches her hands out towards her mother as the anaesthetic takes effect.

'You are already perfect, my Katherine,' her mother whispers as Katherine is taken behind closed doors.

The theatre team prepare, inject, monitor. Saline infiltrates Katherine's smooth, elastic skin selected as the donor site. The skin is stretched tightly, but not too tightly. The pressure is even, the cutting blade positioned as the Professor determines the depth of the cut. Slicing the skin strip to exactly the right thickness, he collects the vital skin he needs. Blood, drips, gauze, forceps ... the medical team work carefully. The Professor slices tissue from her thigh sculpting it with all the detail of an artist fashioning plaster. Katherine's face is cut open. Perspiration drips along his surgical mask as the Professor works, reinventing the side of Katherine's face.

The surgery is slow and methodical, requiring intense concentration. Exhausted from the hours of surgery, the Professor finally closes the wounds.

Recovery. Stabbing pain forces Katherine into temporary wakefulness. She opens her eyes and sees her mother sitting beside her. 'Mama.' She reaches for her. The nurse injects pethidine. Nausea. Katherine slips in and out of consciousness.

The days are disturbed, filled with slow recovery. Katherine doesn't even pretend to smile when the

Professor checks her but she knows. *I'll get better. The pain will go. I'm so tired of this.* She tries to turn on her side but the stabbing pain in her head makes her gasp. *When will it end? When? I want to blame someone. Mum? Rachel? My father? Me? Who? I hate this. I can't even dream about being Beauty. I'm the Beast. I don't want to be the Beast. A beast, beast, beast ...*

Every four hours the nurse changes the fluid in the drip. Another nurse flashes her torch through the ward, checking patients.

As her mother wets Katherine's forehead with a hand towel, she speaks to her softly. *'Bambina, bambina,* it will be over soon. Soon. Soon.'

Her mother wakes up, startled by the clank of a metal bucket. 'Sorry,' the cleaner says as he mops under the bed. Katherine opens her eyes, then closes them. The hospital routine irritates her today. She turns away when her mother speaks to her, and pretends to be asleep when the nurse comes in. Rachel rings and her mother speaks to her, but Katherine doesn't want to talk. She rolls onto her side and watches the morning drag into midday, then afternoon.

The Professor and his team arrive in the late afternoon. 'How are you, Katherine?'

'Better. I've been waiting,' she stammers.

Her mother is waiting too.

The Professor nods. 'I expect you're nervous, Katherine. But we have to give some time for healing to start.'

*I just want to know. I don't want to wait any more. It's like I've been waiting all my life.* 'Has it worked?'

'I hope so, Katherine.' He explains the technical details of the operation to the students as he carefully unbandages a small section. The Professor flushes slightly. He takes a deep breath. 'All right, let's see.'

The Professor's team watches expectantly. Her mother and Katherine wait expectantly. Katherine's mother squeezes her daughter's hand. As the Professor bends his head, all they can see is his thinning white hair. Then he looks up. 'It's taking, but we'll know more in a few days.'

'Can I see it? Can I?'

'Not yet. Not until we take off the bandages. No congratulations until then. You take it easy until those bandages are off.'

'I will. I will.'

Katherine's mother goes back to work. She doesn't get her promotion. 'You took off too much time,' they say. 'We need someone more reliable.'

Every afternoon her mother and Rachel visit Katherine. Jessie comes twice. Then one morning there is a man at the end of her bed. He's got reddish hair and is tall. Katherine only half recognises her father at first. He hands her a large box of chocolates. 'How are you?'

She takes the chocolates. A sense of another time overtakes her. *Is this unfinished business? Am I three again? Is that you visiting when Mum is out of the room? Rachel was so angry at you.*

'Did the operation work out, Katherine?'

'I'm not sure. Maybe.' There's silence.

His shifts uncomfortably at the foot of the bed. 'So, I hope you're feeling all right.'

'I'm all right.' *I am you know. Mum, Rachel and me. We're all right.* 'I'm glad we met in the cafe.'

'I am too.'

'The flowers for my birthday were nice. Pink roses.' There's a long silence. 'Mum grows roses. They're lovely.'

*Your pink roses died and I had to throw them out. Mum's roses are there all year — stalks, new leaves, buds. They are always there for me, like Mum.*

'Your mother was always a great gardener.'

'She works at it. You have to take care of a garden, if it's going to grow.' *You didn't take care of me and help me grow, did you?* 'Thanks for coming to visit.' Katherine looks at him. *You don't drink now and you're sorry, but I can't give you anything. It's too late. I'm glad you like where you live and what you do. A geologist in the outback. But it has nothing to do with me.* 'If you want to ring me sometimes, it's all right. And send a card. I'd like a card.' She waits for a moment. 'But I don't want you to visit the hospital again. It would hurt Mum and Rachel.' *And they're too important to me.*

He stands there not saying anything. When the tea lady arrives, Katherine turns away from him and asks for coffee and biscuits.

'Well, I better go then.'

'Yes. Thanks for the chocolates.' *I'm glad you visited. I needed to see you. Now I need you to leave.*

Tomorrow is the day. Bandages off. Katherine tries to sleep but she calls out in her dreams. The nurse flashes a light over Katherine's bed, startling her.

'Sorry if I frightened you. Are you all right?'

'What time is it?'

'Three in the morning. Get some sleep.'

When she opens her eyes it's suddenly six and the hospital is alive and busy — blood pressures taken, pills distributed, cleaners mopping floors, breakfast trays. Her mother arrives. 'I wanted to make sure I am here before the Professor comes.' She drops her handbag on the bed. 'You look tired, Katherine. You did not sleep well last night?' She's brought the first rose of the season. The rose petals are pink and smooth.

'I slept fine, Mum.'

'I will find a vase.'

The Professor is much earlier than usual. He's accompanied by a large group of doctors. Katherine's mother follows them into the room with the vase.

'So it's time, Katherine. Are you ready?'

She nods. 'Yes, I'm ready.'

He chats with her about surfing, school, what she plans for the holidays until all the bandages are off. Katherine's mother gasps. There is excited talk among the doctors. 'Remember, there's a lot of swelling but it will settle down. There'll need to be more work done on it too.' The Professor rubs his chin.

Taking a deep breath, she asks, 'Can I wear my hair up?'

'Not yet. There are a few more things to do first, but I hope one day.'

*I will wear my hair up.* 'Thank you. Thank you.'

The doctors leave, talking about the surgery. 'Mum, Mum, get your mirror. I want to see. I want to see.' She rifles through her mother's handbag. 'I can't wait. Here it is.' The morning sunlight hits the glass as she flips open the mirror case. 'It's too bright.' She turns her back to the sunlight. 'I'm going to be normal like you always said. Beautiful, perfect. Perfect me.'

She lifts her long hair away from her face, pulling it so that it hangs down on her left side. Then she holds the mirror so that it reflects the side of her face. She holds the mirror very still. Very still. From her red, distorted skin, there is a thick, pulpy mass like old rubber glued onto the side of her head. Red and misshapen. Like an alien growth.

Katherine stares questioningly at her mother. 'You said I would be beautiful. You said that. You lied to me.' She throws the mirror onto the floor. It crashes into a myriad of splinters.

'You lied. Lied.'

Katherine sobs in her mother's arms.

# CHAPTER TWENTY-TWO

She doesn't dream of Beasts and Beauties. She doesn't dream at all, but the nights are frightening. V.V. Sipos' lines chant like nightmares: 'the hiders, hunching their shoulder, huddled in obscurity'. In the morning, she's exhausted.

'I'm sorry, Mum. You'd never lie to me.' 'Yes, I think everything is going to be great, Professor.' 'Rachel, my face is still swollen. I don't want to show anyone.' 'William, please don't visit. You've got your exams anyway. We'll go out afterwards.' 'No, I can't see you yet, Jessie.'

*What's wrong with me, Pup? I expected something different. Looking into the mirror was awful.* She shakes her head. *It was the shock, that's all. The Professor said it was too early to see. Hey Pup, tell me to shut up. I've got to get myself together. You know, Pup* ... She touches his bald old head. *Your ears are a bit hairy. At least I'll never have hairy ears. But you wait, one day ... I was disappointed. Isn't that a pathetic word? Disappointment. I've had a lot of that. But you know what? I'm not going to hide. Not after everything I've been through. No way.*

Every day she escapes into the bathroom to look in the mirror. She gasps, leaning on the white porcelain basin with its stainless steel taps. Her hair falls like tangled string down her back, but she can't bear to comb it. When Rachel visits, she sits by Katherine's bed and gently teases out the knots, brushing and brushing, making her sister's hair shine.

As Katherine lifts up her hair and looks into the mirror, she catches her breath. *I think the swelling is less. Is it getting better? I think it is.*

Every day, the swelling reduces a little more. *Please, please, let it get better.* Every day it looks a little less red, less alien. *Maybe the Professor's right. It just needs time.* Then, one day, her face starts to look like hers. Katherine stares motionless into the mirror. *Are you part of me? Is that my skin? No, you're still red, imperfect.* Katherine nervously touches her face, edging her fingers carefully under her hair, over her ear. *I'm scared.* She traces her face with the tip of her finger, then with all her fingers. It's still swollen, but better. Katherine smiles.

'There will be more surgery, Katherine. You'll be in and out of hospital, Katherine,' the Professor says.

*There's still more to be done.* Katherine closes her hands tightly. *But it looks better and maybe ... beautiful. Well, one day. Just a few more months. By the end of the year, it'll be better. By Christmas, it'll be better.*

When Katherine arrives home from the hospital Rachel is waiting at the front door. 'I'm back,' she announces.

'Does that mean you'll keep the bathroom tidy?' Rachel asks. 'Just joking. I know that's impossible. I missed you.'

'Me too.'

Their mother smiles. 'I also.'

'So, Katherine, when do I see it?'

'Remember my face is still swollen, but it's improving all the time.'

'No excuses.'

'You're right. No excuses.' Katherine pulls back her hair.

Her mother touches Katherine's hand.

Rachel hugs her sister. She whispers into her ear. 'It's getting there.'

Her grandparents phone to congratulate Katherine. 'It is wonderful about your surgery. We will see you at Christmas.' Then Nonna talks about the cold weather in her village. 'Autumn is starting, and the leaves of the oak trees are yellow and lovely, but it is cold. There is snow already in the mountains.'

'I promise it will be hot here. You and Grandpapa can swim.'

'Yes, Grandpapa enjoys swimming. Ah, was it good, the jumper I knitted for you to keep warm in hospital?'

'The bedjacket? Oh, yes, it was great, Nonna.' *Stuffed in the back of my cupboard.*

Grandpapa takes the phone, but his English isn't very good and he speaks disjointedly about the fishermen and big catches. He doesn't take his boat out so much any more and there is loss in his voice for the passing of a part of his life. Katherine sympathises, but it seems so far away. When her mother gets onto the phone, it's different. As a girl, she went with her father on fishing expeditions into the Mediterranean Sea. She talks as though it's still her home.

After the phone call Katherine asks, 'I've always wondered, Mum. Why didn't you go back to Italy after my father left?'

'A lot of times I wanted to,' she reflects. 'Your nonna and grandpapa wanted me to go home. They had forgiven me.' She looks at Katherine.

'So why did you stay here?'

She hesitates. 'My pride. When I left my college in the middle of my studying and ran away with my handsome foreigner, I told my parents that they knew nothing.' Her lips tremble a little. 'I was the one who knew nothing.

'Then you were burnt and there was so much to do. I had to be in a big city for the doctors, the hospitals. There were no such hospitals in the village.'

'But it's been hard for you, Mum.'

'Yes. We now live here. You have grown up here. This is our home.' She leans towards Katherine and gently kisses her cheek. 'You are going out tonight with William to see the basketball. I know it is hard for you to go out so soon.'

'I'll just have to wear my hair down for a little longer. I can't wait,' she presses her lips together, 'to be fully healed. You wouldn't want me to wait, would you, Mum?'

'I am very proud of you, Katherine.'

There's the sound of a horn beeping. 'That's William. Got to go.'

The Valiant has been waxed and polished and sparkles in places. In other places no amount of waxing and polishing can help. The chrome bumper bar is tied on with rope so that it doesn't fall off. William plans to work on the car, do a few essential repairs, like fixing the leaking radiator and spluttering carburettor. 'Your car looks terrific,' Katherine says as she jumps in.

'It'll sound terrific too, after I've worked on it this weekend.'

There are no difficult silences. All their talking on the phone has made them comfortable with each other. He asks about her surgery.

'It'll be perfect by Christmas.' *Perfect? As perfect as it can be and then I'll have to just accept whatever I am.* She brushes her hand over William's.

They chat about the pressure of exams for a while, then they talk about surfing and the basketball game tonight. 'Do you mind going for drinks after the game?' William adds, 'Jessie and Greg are coming.'

'That'll be fun. Jessie said Greg's playing tonight.'

'He's made it into the A's, which is great,' William says. 'Marc's playing as well.'

*Marc?* 'As long as it's not too late, it'll be fine to go.' *Marc. Paper-bag girl. It doesn't even hurt now. And this girl will have a proper face. Not perfect, but better. Won't need a paper bag, but that doesn't even matter because guess what? William kissed me. No paper bag required.* Katherine settles back in the roomy car seat with its frayed edges. 'These old seats are really comfortable.'

Katherine looks out of the window as William drives alongside the bushland reserve. 'I'm going to start training on the track again,' she says. I need to be fit for lifesaving and I like the run anyway.' A tingle shivers down her back and she folds her arms around herself. 'Maybe I'll notice the echnidas this time.'

William puts on a Beach Boys cassette. 'Surfin' USA', 'California Girls', 'Rhonda' . . .

'You're really an OLD surfer, I can hear that.' She hides a smile behind her hand.

'Hey, are you laughing at me?'

'I wouldn't do that. Aren't those songs from the sixties and seventies?'

'They sure are. The Beach Boys do a few new songs occasionally these days, but I like their early music. It's what surfing is about. Riding the waves, parties, having mates, girls and a good time. Aren't you sick of the deep and meaningful stuff that's on the radio?'

'I don't mind meaningful. I mind self-pity.'

William swerves around a corner.

'I can't listen to self-pity. Yes, there's pollution, war, family break-ups. But eventually you've got to stop blaming your parents, teachers, the government, whoever. Do something yourself.' Katherine rocks in time to 'Surfin Safari'.

*You have to believe in yourself. Change what you're able to change, but accept what you are. No blame.*

The Sports Complex is crowded with basketball players, coaches, spectators, kids running around with ice-creams. The microphone blares directions for teams to get ready. Katherine sees Jessie waving at them. Motioning them to come up into the stands. She is wearing Greg's team's colours. Red ribbons in her hair and a red T-shirt. 'I wonder who you support,' Katherine teases.

There's the whistle. The game begins. The referee tosses the ball into the air. Marc grabs the ball, beating the Blue Centre to it. Throwing, dribbling, defending the ball is fast and furious. Greg shoots for a basket. He gets it in. Jessie out-screams the other supporters cheering on the sidelines. The Blues have the ball now and it's traveling fast up the court to their basket. A Blue player barges into Marc, who falls. The referee blows his whistle hard. 'Foul,' he calls out. Marc gets a free throw. He throws it to Greg, who dribbles it fast down the court. Then a high jump shot. Another basket. The Reds are fast. The Blues can't compete against the high speed offensive attack. Another basket. The come-back with a strong defence …

Half-time. Greg leans against the railing, breathing heavily. His face is red, like his hair. Marc keeps moving with barely controlled energy. T-shirts are stained with sweat. Water from plastic bottles drip down faces. The coaches are in separate corners, directing new strategies, identifying opposition weaknesses. The concentration is intense.

Half-time's over. A Blue player passes the ball to a team-mate. Marc intercepts, steals the ball, dribbling it up the court, then a Blue … Red … Blue battling … up and down … a fury of movement and energy. The Red team defend fiercely. The Blues can't get the ball past. The Blue forward isn't successful and the ball travels past him. Goal for Reds. Goal for Blues. Goal for Red. Goal for Reds. Cheering … cheering … cheering …

The Reds win with a final score of 52–38. There are the obligatory congratulations from the Blue team, but they aren't happy. In front of everyone, the Blue's coach verbally attacks the Centre. 'You didn't concentrate. Can't you play? You let the team down. You … You …' Katherine looks away because she doesn't want to see the Blue Centre flushed with humiliation. She shudders. *Coach, it's not the Centre who's let the team down. It's you. If you make someone feel useless, then how can he ever achieve anything?*

William takes Katherine's hand. 'Great game.'

'Great game.' Her swimming coach flits into her thoughts. 'I'm glad we're supporting the Reds.'

Jessie can't stop talking about the game until Katherine gives up. 'Yes, we now know Greg is the best basketball player of all time.'

'Very funny.' But nothing can deflate Jessie's good mood.

They wait for Greg and Marc to come out of the change rooms. They leave the Sports Complex together. Greg has his arm around Jessie as they cross the road and walk to the strip of small shops. Marc's meeting a few friends at the pub. William's still holding Katherine's hand. The small shops are closed except for the Laundromat with its glaring light. Washing machines whirl in their cleaning cycle while two men wait inside at separate ends of the Laundromat. Katherine holds William's hand tighter. *They seem so alone. I've got so much, haven't I?*

They arrive at the corner hotel. It's old-fashioned with a covered awning held up by straight timber poles. People spread out of the pub onto the footpath. Katherine and her friends squeeze in between girls in black and guys in jeans. There's a jazz singer on the piano. William gets the first round.

'A light beer for me,' Marc says. 'I need it after that. But only light. Don't want to ruin my fitness.'

'That's a change,' William laughs.

'If you want to win, you've got to give up some things.' He pretends to punch William in the arm. 'Like full beer.'

William brings back drinks. 'Have a try of my beer, Katherine.'

She looks at it. 'Why not?' Taking a sip, she starts giggling.

'What's the joke?'

'Nothing.' *I feel like a naughty girl with beer. I think I need Mum's approval. No, I don't. I need her support, but it's my decision now. Anyway, we drank Italian wine together, didn't we, Mum?*

Jessie listens to Greg retelling every move on the basketball court. Katherine smiles and listens for a while. She watches Marc. *You've changed. I can't believe it was really you who told me to hide. That no one could love me. You wouldn't now, would you? We're friends.*

'Saturday will be my last game,' Marc says. 'After that it's study. Final exams.'

'There won't be many pub nights for any of you for a while.' Jessie finishes her drink.

'Can't wait till it's all over,' Greg adds.

Marc drinks his beer. 'It's hard to believe we've nearly done thirteen years at school.'

'The formal will be one great party.' William looks at Katherine.

After the second beer, Marc puts his glass down on the table. He smiles at Katherine. 'I'm ready to go.

Anyone else coming?' A few stay on, but Greg and Jessie make their way outside. William and Katherine follow.

The old Valiant is waiting for them in the car park. Katherine pretends to hug it, making William laugh. In the car, William puts on the radio. They both smile when a surfing song comes on as he drives Katherine home.

'I guess we'll both be pretty busy for the next few months, William.'

'We probably won't have a chance to see much of each other for a while.' He hesitates. 'I may as well ask you now. Would you like to come with me to my formal?'

The surfing song echoes through the car.

*. . . do you love me?*
*come on, come on, come on,*
*surfin' girl.*

He glances at her. 'I couldn't take anyone else.'

*surfin' girl*
*I love the way you walk*
*I love the way you talk.*

Hazel eyes. *I knew I always loved them.*

*do you love me?*
*do you surfin' girl?*
*I love you.*

'Yes, I'd like to go to the formal with you, William.'

CHAPTER TWENTY-THREE

The next months are like the coloured confetti thrown at a wedding. Bits and pieces of school, Rachel, surf-lifesaving, her mother, friends and William float fragmented over the hospital with its veil of surgery.

The garden blooms in the warmth of summer. Butterflies flutter browns and blues between roses. Only the worn paling fence separates the spread of colour. Birds of paradise, kangaroo paw, pink roses, marigolds spread from the verandah right to the back fence, meeting the dusty green bush. Rosellas peck at the baskets of seeds hanging on the gums.

Katherine and Jessie lie under the trees on a checked blanket. They drink water from bottles. It's hot and they pick at the grass. 'Greg came for dinner last week. Dad sort of approves of him because Greg plans to do Law. Mum just wants peace and quiet, so she likes anyone.' Jessie rolls onto her back. 'But what matters is that I really like him.'

'Are you going to tell me, Jessie?'

She nods. 'I want to. I know you'll keep it a secret.' Jessie's blonde hair glistens in the afternoon sun and her eyes are tender as she tells her friend about lying under the trees with the moon softening the night and how his hands touched her and it felt natural . . .

*William's touched my face. Kissed me. I loved his hands stroking my hair, but when he touched my shoulder, my arms, there were scars. How can he touch me?* Katherine shudders.

'It was half an accident in the end. We'd got so close a lot of times.'

*I saw the love mark on your breast that time you crept into my room.*

'It was different when he started to push. He wanted me so much and he tried to slow down. It hurt. If it hadn't been Greg, I would have been scared.'

*Scared. I know what that is. Sometimes I'm brave. But I understand scared.*

'It doesn't hurt any more. I'm not scared any more.' Jessie reaches for Katherine's hand and presses it. 'Making love is beautiful. I think I love Greg.'

There are more grafts on the side of her face, more redefining. Katherine misses school. *I'm nearly there. Just a bit longer.* The teachers send assignments home. *I'm nearly there. Just.* The Coordinator gets a time extension for the completion of the university entrance exam. *I'm nearly there.* Nausea and recovery. *Nearly there. Nearly.*

The back doors are open, letting the late spring breeze filter through the house. Dressed in a black dinner suit and a plain, white silk shirt, William sits in a chair waiting. Katherine's mother hands him a small box. 'She will be here soon.'

Rachel does last-minute touches to Katherine's hair. She threads a thin blue ribbon through it.

'Can you see the scars?'

'You look pretty, Katherine.'

'But there are still scars.' *I'm scared. Why am I always scared inside?*

'Go on. William's waiting.'

Katherine looks at her sister. 'I love you, Rachel.' She takes a breath, glances at Rachel, then opens her bedroom door. William is holding a white gardenia. He looks up as she walks into the room. She smiles at him.

He smiles too.

The satin of her pale blue dress shimmers in the evening light. Nervously, she touches her gold necklace with its initial pendant. Katherine's hair is half swept up.

He moves towards her and hands her the gardenia. Katherine ties it around her wrist. 'It's lovely.'

He hands her a small box. 'Your mother wanted me to give you this.'

She unwraps it slowly. There is some tissue paper inside. Opening the paper, she sees them. *I can't believe it. They're so beautiful.*

William strokes her face. She wants to move backwards, but doesn't. The small earrings match her necklace. They sparkle as he slides them onto her ears.

The days are busy with preparations for Christmas. The turkey is stuffed, the vegetables peeled, sliced and ready for the oven. The ham is in the fridge. It only has to be cut up and the fresh mangoes, pineapples and fruit displayed around it. King-size prawns and oysters have been bought and the sauces made. The fridge is overflowing. *Panettone*, sweet cake filled with candied fruit, has been baked and sits cooling on the kitchen table.

The house is festive. The sun beats down on the front window stenciled with snowflakes and a large white Santa. Christmas cards line the mantelpiece. The Professor's card takes pride of place in the centre. The fir tree is decorated with tinsel and baubles. Presents are piled under its branches.

Christmas Eve. Nonna arrives wearing thick stockings, boots and a woollen dress. Grandpapa wears an open shirt and jacket. There is hugging and kissing and their mother cries at the airport.

Nonna and their mother talk all the way home. When they arrive at the house, their mother has to show them everything — her house, garden, the birds that visit, the bush that surrounds them. Then there are photo albums. They pour over the years. Katherine and Rachel before the accident ... the burns, hospital, doctors, the Professor, picnics, the elastic suit and yellow sausage, school, friends, operations ... Nonna and Grandpapa ask to see how Katherine looks now with her hair swept up.

She pulls back her hair, exposing her neck, her face.

'*Bene*, Katherine.' 'Wonderful, Katherine.' They nod, but Katherine can see they don't understand that it is *really* wonderful.

Her mother is smiling. *You understand, don't you, Mum?*

Jetlag finally catches up with Nonna and Grandpapa and they go to sleep in Rachel's room. Rachel complained for days when she was forced to move in with Katherine.

'You just have to accept it. Maybe you'll learn to be messy like me. You're lucky. I've gone off hard rock. It's The Beach Boys now.'

On Christmas morning Nonna is wearing a cotton shift, and she's changed her heavy boots for sandshoes. Grandpapa has already gone local and is wearing shorts, a T-shirt and joggers. Christmas carols play in the background as they sit around the tree to give and receive presents. Katherine gives her mother and Rachel their favourite perfumes but the gifts seem trivial. *Nothing could ever compare to what I've got already.* There are presents of clothing, soaps, diaries, sweets and money from Grandpapa and Nonna.

At Christmas lunch Grandpapa carves the turkey. Katherine can't remember anyone except her mother doing that. Grandpapa makes jokes in broken English. Katherine and Rachel laugh even though they only half understand them. Their mother and Nonna laugh. There is wine at the table, but Grandpapa drinks two beers. There has never been beer in their house before. Grandpapa holds Nonna's hand and calls her *cara*, but he calls Rachel, *Principessa* — Princess. And Katherine, *Bellezza* — Beauty.

In the late afternoon, William drives up in his Valiant. Grandpapa is very interested in the car and looks under the bonnet with him. His broken English doesn't seem to matter when they discover they both love the sea. As they drink beer together, they talk about big seas and currents and the vagaries of the ocean.

It's early evening by the time William and Katherine get the chance to walk in the garden together. 'I hope you like this present,' she says. 'I looked around for it for ages.'

He unwraps the surfing book. 'Katherine. You really know me. Thanks.'

She shakes her head when she opens The Beach Boys CD he's bought her. There is another package with it. 'What's in this? I bet it's sand.'

'No, you lose that bet.'

She opens the box. The silver charm bracelet tinkles in her hands. Taking it from her, William clasps it around her wrist. Slowly he runs his hand up her arm, drawing her to him.

'You know I don't care about your burns. They're part of you and that makes them okay.'

*I want to be perfect. I'm not, am I? Even after all the surgery.* 'Doesn't it matter, William?' *Do you really mean that?*

He pushes her hair away from her face and kisses her gently.

From her bedroom window Katherine sees kookaburras on the clothesline. She sees her mother's roses and smells the scents of the bush. Butterflies defy their fragile wings and dance in the breeze, *like me.*

She turns to look at Rachel, who is sound asleep. Pup is on Katherine's bed. *I can't explain how much I love you, Mum, Rachel. I'm lucky, there are so many people in my life. The Professor and everyone in the hospital. Jessie and Liz, my school friends, Mr Roberts, even the Coordinator. There's William. I think I love him. And this Christmas, Nonna and Grandpapa are here.*

*I've got things I want to do. Lifesaving. Championships, I hope. Work at Cafe Smooth. That'll give me money for holidays. Study. I'm going to be a doctor. I just know it.* She wipes away tears. *Why am I crying? Professor, I'm going to be a hero like you.*

*There'll always be some scars. Not as many now. I can live with it.*

*I'm not so scared any more. I don't feel like the Beast any more.*

*Not now.*

Not ever.

There is no word that adequately describes someone who has been burnt severely, treated and returned to the community. The nearest is 'survivor' because it implies suffering, endurance, and eventual resumption of a normal or near-normal life.

Every survivor has a story. Often the story is of interest, and even more often, instructive. This book is the story of a burn survivor, and it is both interesting and instructive. It explores the complex areas of the emotional impact of a burn on the individual and the family while giving insight into the world of hospitals, patients and doctors. It traces the development of the personality from insecurity and relative isolation to a healthier level of self-esteem that enables the individual to form balanced relationships with family and friends. It shows how the inner person can triumph over a preoccupation with surface scars and know that basic values of commitment, caring and trust are more important than the texture of the skin.

The book has relevance outside the narrow circle of burn survivors and their families. It shows the ebb and flow of emotions that affect us all, particularly in the transition between childhood and adulthood, and how parenting and family life make these bearable.

Those of us who are involved in the world of burns know how survivors need help from time to time, but slowly develop a depth of character and an inner strength which is rarely seen in others. Like tempering steel, the process of passing through the fire helps make a person of exceptional quality. This book captures these subtleties for the reader, and gives a stunning insight.

DR HUGH MARTIN

*PRESIDENT OF THE AUSTRALIAN AND NEW ZEALAND BURN ASSOCIATION and HEAD OF THE BURN UNIT, THE CHILDREN'S HOSPITAL, WESTMEAD, NSW.*